THIS IS TO CERTIFY THAT...
Summer
Boydstun
(YOUR NAME)
is becoming
Radically
REVVED UP
HOME
FIX-IT
by using
the ideas
in this
REV-UP
KIT!

Dedication

This book is dedicated to Matthew, our first radically REVVED-UP kid! He has certainly revved-up our lives. There's more joy, more action and more love!

Acknowledgements

Many thanks to Roger Harvey for his wonderful illustrations, great ideas and excellent writing skills. I really appreciate his friendship and his commitment to helping kids through his work.

Warm thanks to Dr Shayne Yates for his input during the development stages.

Unlimited thanks to both my parents and Colin's parents for their endless support and encouragement in all that Colin and I do. The achievement of this book also belongs to them.

The biggest thanks are for my fantastic husband Colin who is also my partner in business. His vision to help youth constantly challenges me to expand my thinking. Not only is he my best friend, he's my greatest encourager and fan. Only God could have given me such a wonderful partner for life. I thank the Lord too!

Published in Australia
by
Cassette Learning Systems Pty Ltd

First published in July, 1993
Printed by McPherson's Printing Group
Melbourne
AUSTRALIA

ISBN 0 646 14468-5

Totally inspiring for young achievers!

Lisa McInnes-Smith
with
Roger Harvey

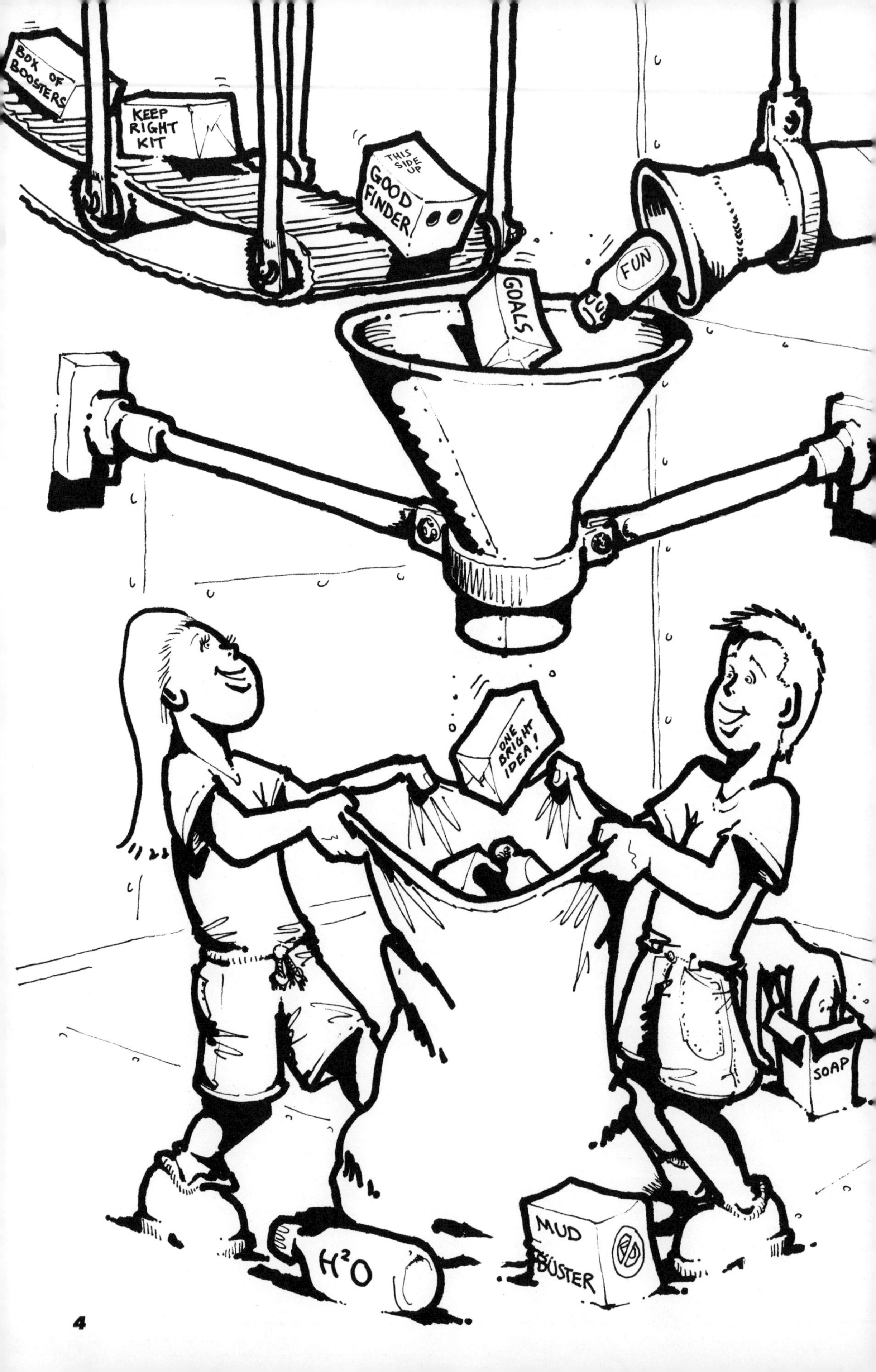
BOX OF BOOSTERS
KEEP RIGHT KIT
THIS SIDE UP
GOOD FINDER
FUN
GOALS
ONE BRIGHT IDEA!
SOAP
MUD BUSTER
H²O

Contents

*** denotes 'Time Out!'**

HOME
DUTY
ROSTER
ATHLETICS
CLUB
MEETS
MANNERS
GUIDE
GREEN
PEACE
BIRTHDAYS
LIST

A word from Lisa ...

Eight years ago I had a wonderful dream that changed my life. My dream was to positively affect the lives of one million teenagers. At the time of publication of this book, it is close to being a dream come-true. The journey this dream has taken me on has transformed my life in ways I never thought possible. Many of the lessons I have learnt on my journey are included in this book.

On the 1st of September, 1992, my life (As well as my husband Colin's!) was radically changed by the birth of our first child Matthew John. Since then I have learnt so much more about kids! I have come to really understand that kids are more valuable and more precious than anything else in the world.

I have a desire in my heart to share with you the good things that I know. Commit yourself to this book and I am certain you will become the best God-Made-Human you can be.

I pray you have as much fun learning from this book as I have had in writing it!

With love,
Lisa

HARLEY

Chapter ONE

YOUR AMAZING MACHINE!

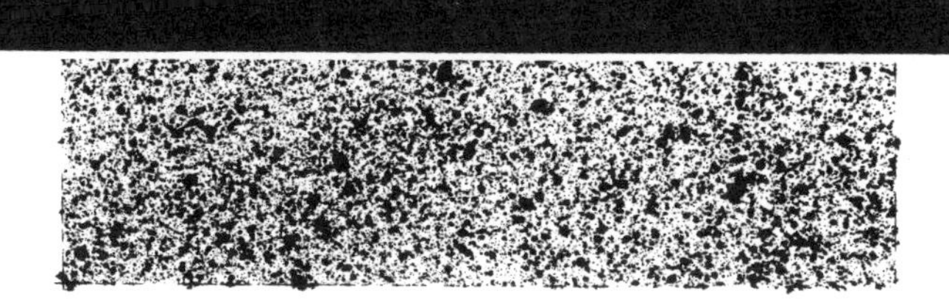

YOUR AMAZING

Congratulations! You are the proud owner of a single-seater, naturally fuelled, God-Made-Human (GMH) body.
This amazing machine is the vehicle which will carry you through life's great journey.
Although not new (you have owned it since birth), your GMH body is young, strong and bursting with possibilities! It should run well for the next 70 to 95 years. Take care of your 'human vehicle' as it is the only one you will own for as long as you live. (Spare parts like hearts and livers are rare and expensive.) Your GMH vehicle needs wholesome fuel, lots of exercise, plenty of rest and loving care. Be careful where you 'drive' it. Keep your engine in top condition and enjoy the lifelong journey!

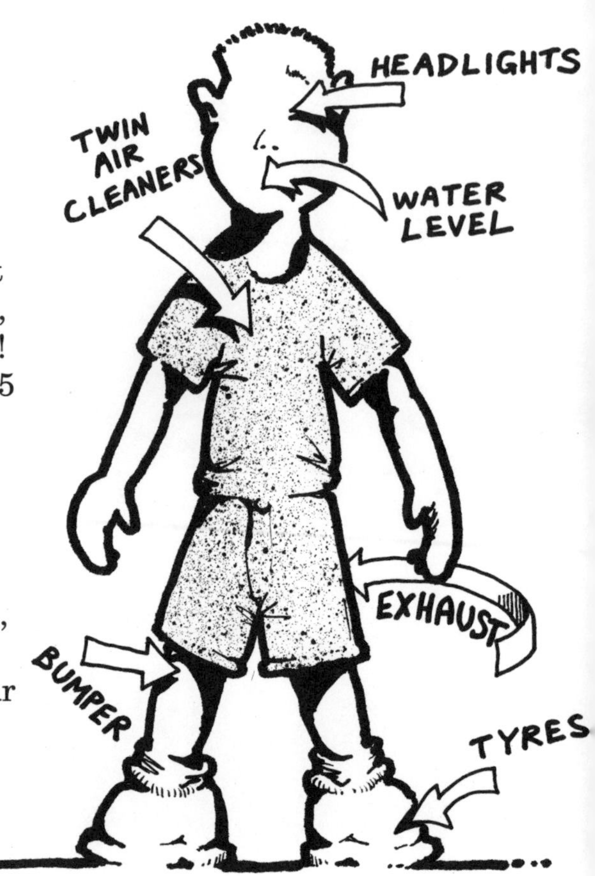

MACHINE!

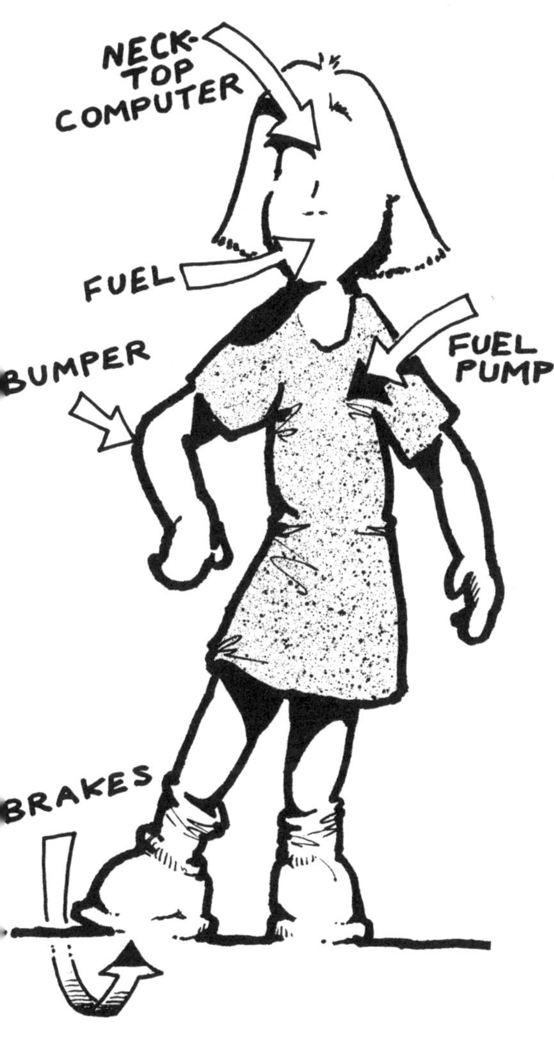

The Mighty GMH

Just as a motor car body hides and protects the engine, so your human body hides and protects your GMH engine.
When God made you He created some wonderful body parts that make you very special. Here are a few which help you to keep revved-up.

The Neck-Top Computer

Your head contains the powerful neck-top computer called the brain. Your brain is the most complex structure in the universe. It houses thirteen billion nerve cells. There are more than three times as many cells in each GMH brain as there are people on the earth. The brain has filed away every sound, taste, smell and action you have experienced since the day you were born. It does not respond well to poor treatment like alcohol, cigarettes or drugs. When used properly, it becomes smarter every day!

The Fuel Pump

Your fuel pump (or heart) beats approximately 115,000 times each day, pumping blood and fuels through more than 60,000 miles of veins, arteries and tubing. Regular exercise strengthens the pump. Junk food and fatty foods cause it to wear out early.

"You cannot be intelligent and smoke at the same time."
- Dr John Tickell

The Twin Air Cleaners

Your twin air cleaners (or lungs) just love exercise. They are made up of more than six hundred million pockets of folded flesh. Even in polluted air they work to take in life - giving oxygen and get rid of gaseous wastes. Smoking damages these filters and should be avoided at all times.
As you know, the twin air cleaners do not work underwater. The God-Made-Human will stop working if submerged for long. (You should learn to swim.)

WHAT DO

You Are Special!

Have you noticed that, just like cars, people 'drive around' in bodies of many different sizes, shapes and colours? One person isn't better than another, just different to others. No two God-Made-Humans are exactly the same, but each one is very special.
When God created you He joined two cells. With the combination that He had at His command, He could have created three hundred thousand billion different GMHs. But He chose to create you! You are one of a kind!
So how would you describe your body to a friend? What makes your vehicle stand out in a crowd?

Let's see how the authors describe themselves:

LISA
long blonde hair
fair skin and freckles
long skinny legs
special marks
crooked middle finger
stitched-up eyelid

ROGER
thick spiky hair
tanned skin
huge feet
special marks
missing fingertip (ouch!)
big nose

YOU DRIVE?

"It is not what we have that counts, but what we do with what we have."

Challenge

Your Turn!

It's your turn now! List some points that describe your body. Don't forget your 'special marks'!

body description

Summer
long brown hair
Freckles and light skin
tall and athiaiete

special marks

brith mark

Second opinion!

Now ask someone else to describe your body.

special marks

People who can appreciate their good points and funny parts, tend to enjoy driving their GMH more. Did you see the good in you?
There is good in everyone, so ask someone if you can't see it yourself.

WHAT MAKES

Let's take a closer look at the value of you as a God-Made-Human. There have been about seventy billion GMHs on planet Earth since the beginning of time and yet there has never been anyone exactly like you. Do you think this makes you valuable?

QUESTION
What makes something valuable?
ANSWER
Something is valuable when:

1. **Someone wants it very much.**
2. **It can't be easily replaced.**
3. **Someone is prepared to pay a high price for it.**
4. **It is loved.**

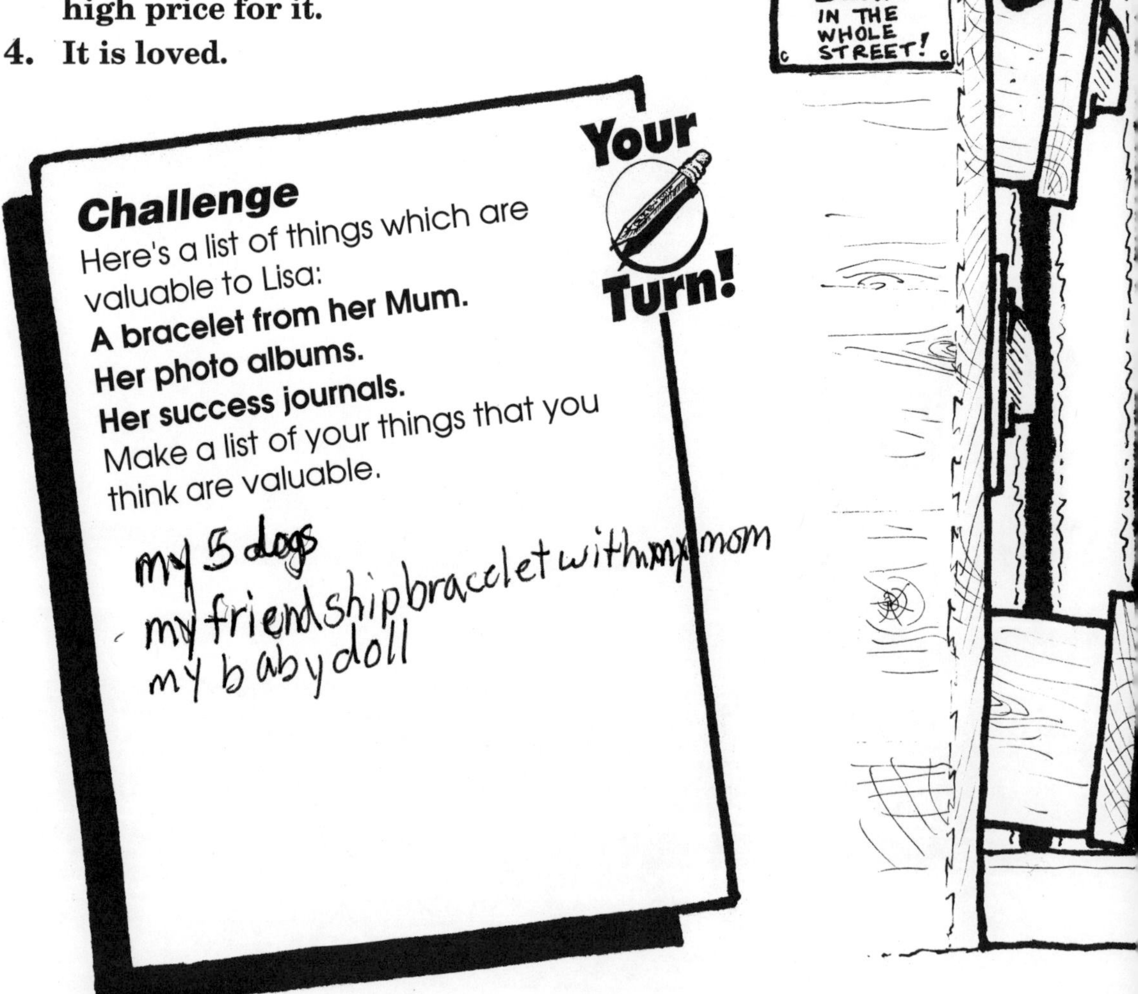

SOMETHING VALUABLE?

"Valuable means worth a lot."

True Value

Are the things you've listed worth a lot of money?

Are they worth a lot to you because someone important gave them to you?

Are they worth a lot because they took a long time to collect?

As you can see, only the owner of a possession knows its real value. If you wouldn't want to lose a special treasure, then you probably think that it's valuable.
Now, what about **you?**
Are you valuable? yes!!

HOW VALUABLE

Challenge

Try This!

Let's put **YOU** to the test.
How valuable are you?
Answer these three questions to find out:

1. **Does someone want YOU very much?**

WHO wants you?

WHY do they want you?

"When we know our own worth, there's no need to tell others how good we are.

(Compare your answers to Lisa
on page 154)

ARE YOU?

2. **Can YOU be easily replaced?**

YES  **NO** 

Because I'm one of a kind !!

3. **Is someone prepared to pay a lot for you?**

YES  **NO**

WHO would pay a lot for you?

my parates

WHY would they pay a lot for you?

They pay a lot for me and them,

4. **Are you loved?**

GETTING A HEAD

...in drawing

We interrupt this book to bring you a quick lesson on *"HOW TO DRAW A FACE"*

NOSE

Add second hole

Add a round end

Add two edges to holes

MOUTH

Add line of bottom lip

Add line at each end of mouth

Bend them to make a smile (RE-DRAW)

EYE

Add circle

Add second circle

Add white dot (not quite in centre.)

HEAD

Head

Swell the cheeks (RE-DRAW)

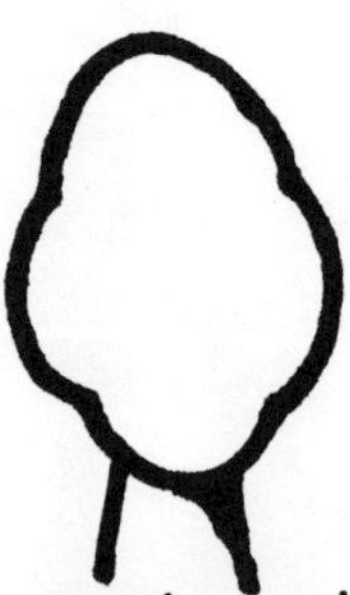

Add neck. Point the chin a little (RE-DRAW)

Draw all bits (RE-DRAW)

Hmmm. Funny looking head. We obviously need to do some more work on it ... Let's have another look at the eyes.

Time Out!

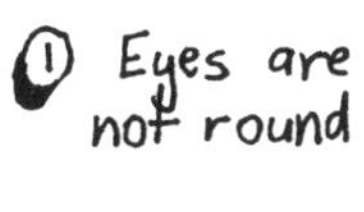

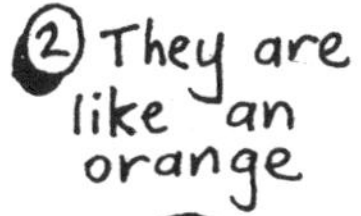

3 They have a line

4

(RE-DRAW)
Add all bits.

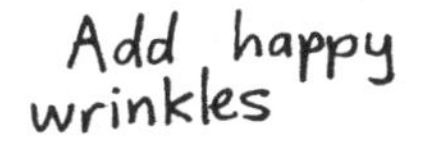

Curve lines up to centre

Push lines down to nose

RE-DRAW HEAD
(MOOD → "ANGRY")

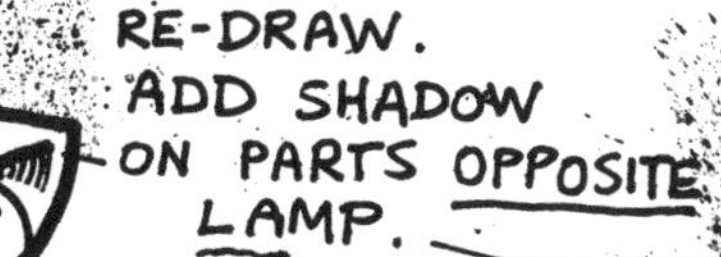

RE-DRAW.
SELECT MOOD: ⇨ EXTRA HAPPY! (MOUTH OPEN...)
ADD WRINKLES...

What's that, you say? Where are the ears? What about the hair, eye-brows, eye-lashes and teeth? Sorry - no more space!

SHOULD YOU

Have you ever noticed that when you feel good about yourself others seem to be nice to you too?
Just as a mirror reflects your image, so does your attitude to yourself reflect how you feel about others. When you hate yourself, you seem to hate everybody else too. When you like being who you are, you can like others too. Remember, you are a great GMH! People will treat you the way you treat yourself.
There may be many things that you do not like about yourself, but you can learn how to like yourself more by learning to spot the good in you. This is called being a **"GOOD-FINDER!"** (created by a wonderful man named Mr. Zig Ziglar).

When you like yourself you are happier, so here are 7 steps to help you:

1. **Be a GOOD-FINDER!**
2. **Speak well of yourself - say positive things about yourself.**
3. **When you receive a compliment, say 'thank-you'.**
4. **Treat your body with respect. (then others will too!)**
5. **Look for the good in others and pay compliments.**
6. **Hang around people who like themselves (and others).**
7. **When you do something good, give yourself some praise.**

"No matter what you've got, be the best you can be with all that you have."

LIKE YOURSELF? ....YES!

Challenge

Now list all the good points you can find in you. Write as many as you can.

GOOD-FINDER List

Examples:
I am caring.
I love my parents.
I am good at basketball.
I bake a great chocolate cake.

I good at showsing dogs.
I good at swiming.
I good at math & science.
I Love my mommy & daddy & friends
I'm good with puppyes and dogs

If you have had a little trouble filling this list, ask your friends and parents to help you. They know your good bits!

When you look for the good in you, you often find more than you expected. It's easy to like yourself when you are a 'GOOD-FINDER'.

WHAT IS THE

You have already described what you look like, but which is more important?

the inside you?

the outside you?

Write down which of these things are **inside** you and which are **outside** you?

Try This!

feelings
jacket
kindness
haircut
fingerprints
love
creativeness
eyes
friendliness
tennis shoes
happiness
intelligence
sun-glasses
humour
caring
backpack
trustworthy
tee-shirt
patience
skin colour
enthusiasm

Read the list again, and this time circle the ones that are really important to you.

Now that you have a better idea of which things are inside and outside, which do you think is more important?

REAL YOU?

"People can see the outside, but not your heart, your thoughts and your courage."

WHAT IS IMPORTANT?

WHAT'S WRONG WITH JIM?
HE DOESN'T TALK MUCH ... BECAUSE NOBODY LIKES HIM.
THAT'S SAD. WHY DON'T THEY LIKE HIM?
...BECAUSE HE DOESN'T TALK MUCH.

I NEVER SEEM TO DO ANYTHING RIGHT.
BUT YOU HAVE A LOT OF FRIENDS AND YOU'RE IN THE SCHOOL TENNIS TEAM... AND YOU ALWAYS DO YOUR HOMEWORK... AND YOUR SCHOOL RESULTS ARE IMPROVING... AND YOU ALWAYS SAY GOOD THINGS ABOUT PEOPLE...
BUT OTHER THAN THAT — I NEVER SEEM TO DO ANYTHING RIGHT.

GOD LOVES

Here's an idea! Imagine yourself in simple clothes, just standing there, alone. Now picture God looking down on you. What do you think He sees? He sees everything! God knows everything about you.
God knows your name.
He knows where you live.
He knows who your parents are.
(He made them too!)
He knows your favourite things.
He knows all the GMHs that you like.
He knows your shoe size.
He knows every thought you have.
He knows when you are happy or sad.
He knows what you will be good at in the future.
He knows where you will holiday.
He even knows which vegetables you don't like! God knows everything about you, and **He loves you just as you are!**
He might not like all the things you say and do, but that will never stop Him loving you. You are one of His kids.

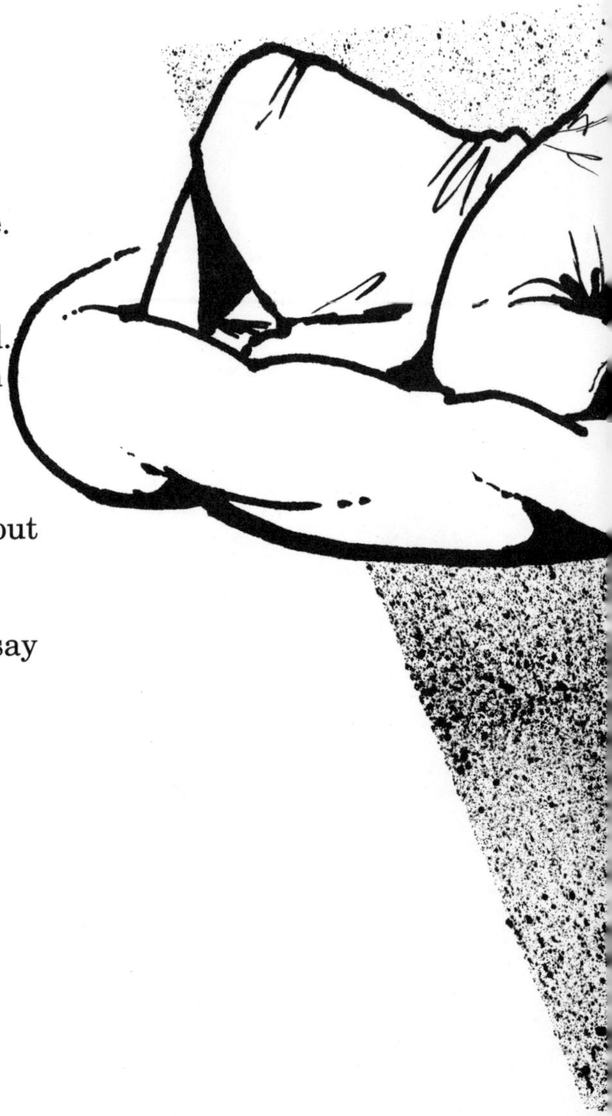

"God speaks to those who want to hear."

YOU!

Who is God?

God is very wise. He has always existed. A long time ago He made all of the natural things you can see. The sun, moon and stars, trees, flowers, animals and birds, rivers, seas and mountains were all made by Him. That is why we often have that deep sense of wonder when we look at the wonderful world around us.

Try This!

How do you feel when you -
Look at the night sky full of bright stars?
See a baby bird in its nest?
Feel the warm breeze on a Summer night?

Just like you, God gets lonely. That is why He made GMHs. The special thing about GMHs is that we were made like Him - so we could relate to Him.

God was (and still is) the first Dad, and He just loves His kids.

Over the years many GMHs forgot about God and did their own thing. So God came to Earth to show GMHs He still wanted to be their friend.

However, some people gave Him a really heavy time. In spite of this, God did many wonderful miracles to make GMHs well and to give them hope for the future.

God knows what it's like to be given a tough time, or to be lonely, or to be in trouble. That is why God can understand and help you - especially when you ask Him.

God has said that He will never leave you alone. He has a great plan for your life. Have a talk to Him about it today.

notes

REV-UP

I feel a little bet better about my self. And I know more about God. I know more about my self.

Chapter TWO

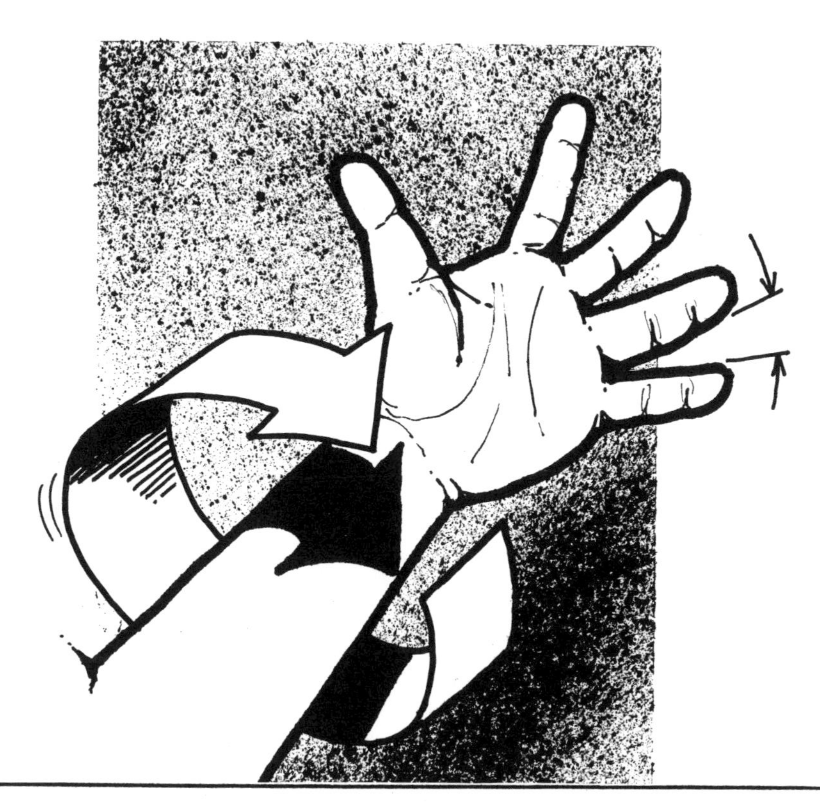

THE GMH BODY-WORKS

hkk

THE GMH SERVICE MANUAL

How to look after your mighty GMH vehicle.

The best 'race cars' are sleek, finely tuned and ready for action. But even the best need regular maintenance and fuel. How about you? Do you need a little attention today? Do you have plenty of vroom and zoom, or are you tired and grumpy? However you feel, it's never too early for a full check-up, service and repair if needed. Park yourself in a chair, read this chapter, and learn how to get the best performance possible from your vehicle.

"Today's choices determine tomorrow's results."

BODY PARTS

Taking care of your GMH body is essential for top performance. Let's take a look at what you can do for some of your main body parts.

Headlights (Eyes)

You get amazing views when your headlights are operated, but they require very special care. Your eyes cannot be replaced so never point them directly into the sun. Don't poke things into others' headlights, and do not rub your own. Water sometimes leaks from the headlights, indicating immediate GMH love and attention is required.

Body Panelling

Your outer surface needs careful attention every day. Keep it fresh and clean by washing well. Protect it from the sun with clothing and sun-block cream.

Bumpers

Bumper knees and elbows break your fall and suffer cuts, grazes and bruises. Life can be pretty tough if you're a GMH bumper. Protect them when you can by wearing a helmet, knee pads, elbowpads, and gloves when doing those exciting sports. (Perhaps God should have given us rubber elbows and knees?)

Exhaust

Empty yourself often. (Go to the toilet!) A GMH will run more smoothly when you don't choke it with a backlog of poisonous waste products. And remember, good manners means controlling your backfires in certain social situations.

Brakes

Regular activity and outdoor games increase your braking ability and balance. Your leg muscles need to be exercised, stretched and put to the test.

Tyres

These cover the feet, help keep the GMH upright and transport it from place to place. Wear well-fitting tyres. Use them for running, jumping and all sorts of games.

IT'S TIME FOR

THE AMAZING MACHINE

Just as a car won't run without fuel, people can't live without food and water. But you're no ordinary vehicle! You are a mighty GMH. You are an amazing machine. You need extra care and several special fuels. You need fuel for the body, fuel for the mind and fuel for the spirit. Let's look at these fuels now.

FUEL FOR THE BODY

Choose only the Best!

The kind of fuel you put in makes a big difference to your GMH performance. Healthy foods are essential. Fruit, vegetables, whole grain breads, pasta, nuts, dairy products, fish and lean meat can turn your GMH into a turbo-charged sports car! Sweets, cakes, lemonade, fatty meats and greasy take-aways add weight and can turn you into a run-down heap! They can make you feel heavy, lazy, and sometimes very sick. They are called 'junk foods' and they will never keep you revved-up.

Water Level

Water is very important for continued peak performance. Most of your body is made up of water (over 80%) so you need to pour lots in for it to run well. Keep the GMH topped up with eight glasses of water each day. Choose to cut down on sweet drinks as these can rust the teeth and add fat to the body. They may taste nice but cause long term problems to your skin, your weight and your health.

FUEL UP!

Food glorious food. What to have next is the question? How often do you think about food? Do you think about healthy food or junk food? Whatever you think about, is often what you look for to eat. If you want to be healthy and full of energy, tell yourself every day that you like healthy food. Say out loud daily:

"I like healthy food."

"I am healthy and I plan to get healthier."

"I am fit and I plan to get fitter."

"I have loads of energy and I plan to get more."

If you don't learn about delicious healthy food now, you could spend the rest of your life being overweight and tired. Choose to learn now!

"It's called 'junk food' because if you eat enough of it, you'll end up on the scrap heap!"

Dr Shayne Yates

"You are what you eat!"

Challenge

Write down the junk foods you are going to cut down. Also write down the foods and drinks you will replace these with.

Junk Foods (To cut down)	Rev-Up Foods (To add)
ice cream	green beens
cake	furitas
coca-cola	milk
candy	water
Sprite	dairy

Challenge

Make a list of the healthy foods and drinks you are going to choose for your GMH at each meal time.

Breakfast	Lunch	Dinner	Snacks
peanut Butter cards, mikk, onige juice	peanut B. and Jelly, chips Juce	up To parints	cheese furits gatrat

Get someone who knows about healthy food to check your lists for you.

Try This!

A SPORTING

By keeping these records, you can easily see the improvement in your growth, strength and fitness. Your records will also be interesting to look back on, in years to come. Make a note of your results once or twice a year and see if you can better them. Hop to it!

Name Summer Boydstun

Year	**Age**	**Height**	**Weigh-In**
97	11	4ft 9.5	92

LEGEND!

Swimming

Date I learnt to swim! ______

YEAR	LAP	Name and length of pool
97	2	fosslpark pool 40ft.

Push-Ups

YEAR	How many I can do
97	three

Running

YEAR	Time for 100 metre run	How Far I can run
97		

Sit-Ups

YEAR	How many I can do
97	26

THE NECK-TOP

FUEL FOR THE MIND

The mind is a fascinating part of your GMH machinery. It is found in your brain and is about the size of a grapefruit. If all the information that you could fit into your mind would fill the space in your house, then all that you're using right now would fit into a shoebox. There is a huge amount of storage space just waiting to be filled with great ideas! And do you know something? No GMH has ever completely filled their neck-top computer. So how does information get into your mind? **You** put it there by talking, reading, watching TV and listening. In fact everything you look at, listen to,experience and say goes into your brain.

Whatever you feed your mind, that is what you will think about. **If you fill it with pictures of happy things, you will think happy thoughts.** The same will happen if you fill your mind with pictures of sad or scary things. You will end up having sad or scary thoughts.
It is up to you to **choose to fill your mind with thoughts that help you feel happy.** Before you learn how to do this, try the next challenge.

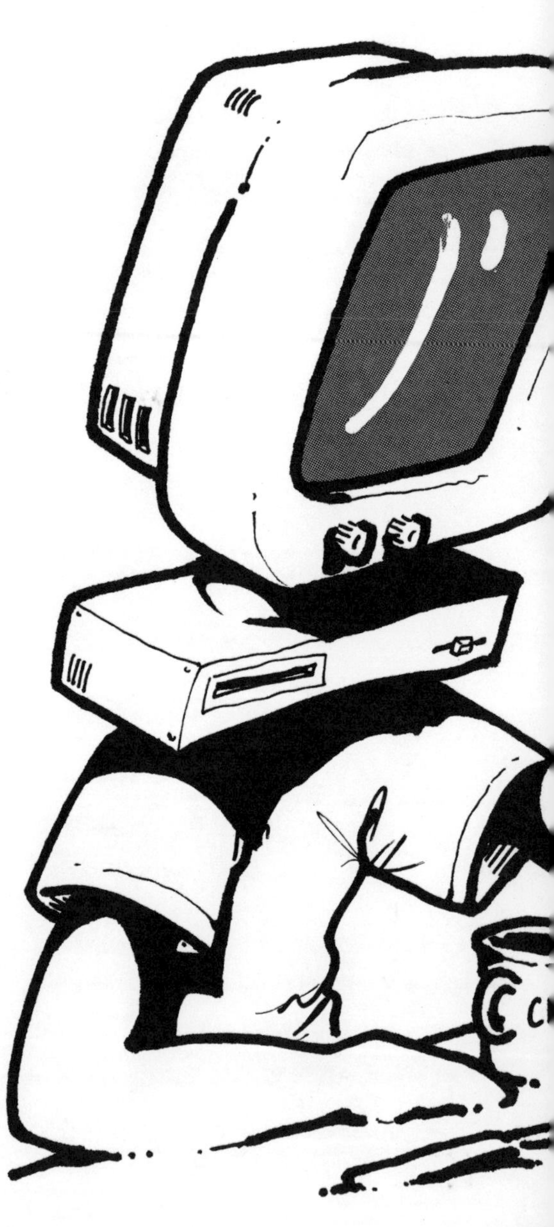

COMPUTER

Challenge

Look at the list below and mark down if you have had many sad or scary thoughts from any of these places:

	Sad	Scary
? Newspapers		
TV Movies	✓	✓
? Computer Games	✓	✓
Books	✓	✓
TV Soaps		✓
Movies	✓	
? TV News		
? Magazines		
Story-telling	✓	✓
Videos	✓	
? TV Ads		
Songs	✓	✓
? Billboards		

Now think of some of the places where you can find thoughts that make you feel good. Write these down and remember to always think happy thoughts.

think of the good parts

"What you put into your mind comes out in your thoughts."

BEING HAPPY

Do you like feeling happy?
How important is it to you to be a happy GMH? What would you be willing to do to be happy? What would you be prepared to give up?
When people are asked "What do you want most in life?", they usually say "I just want to be happy". Have you ever said this? If being happy is so important to you, would you be prepared to work hard at it? Good!
If you want something a lot, it's worth working for.

Take Control

To be happy you must learn how to fill your mind with thoughts that are good for you. This means you must take control of what you put into your GMH mind. There are three ways to do this:

1. **Practice putting good thoughts into your mind.**
2. **Learn how to replace bad thoughts with good thoughts.**
3. **Learn to keep bad thoughts out of your mind.**

GMH Thoughts

"Whatever you think about a lot, you become!"

What is a thought? It is an idea that comes when you think. Thoughts control everything you do and say. You can't do anything or say anything until you think it first. The brain knows what you are going to do and say before your body does it. The brain is the control centre of the body. It is the neck-top computer which runs the GMH.

Your Attitude

If you want to be a happy GMH you need to take control of your thoughts and your attitude. Your attitude is the way you think about things. When many of your thoughts join together they become your attitude. Your attitude then affects everything you do.

'Attitude Pitstop!'

An attitude pitstop is a chance to stop and refuel your mind with positive encouraging statements. These are also known as BOOSTERS. Always start them with "I am", "I have" or "I like". Try these now.

"I am happy."
"I like controlling my thoughts."
"I have an awesome mind."
"I am choosing to be happier everyday."

Feels good, doesn't it!

TAKING CONTROL

"Attitudes are contagious! - Is yours worth catching?"

Let's see how your attitude works. When I say the word homework, what do you think about? If you think "homework is all right", that's having a 'positive' attitude. **A positive attitude is one where your thoughts make the task easier, happier or more fun.**

The opposite to this is a negative attitude. If you think 'I hate homework' these thoughts make the task harder, less pleasant and no fun at all. You spend your time thinking of ways to get out of doing your homework. However, the homework needs to get done whether you like it or not. There are many things you must do in life that you don't like. You do them because they get you the result you want in the long run. So why not choose the attitude that will make the task easier? Why make it harder for yourself by being negative? Remember, you can choose to be a happy GMH. You can choose to be a positive GMH!
In maths we write a negative sign like this - . It usually means 'minus' or 'subtract' or 'take away'.
Read this example: **4 - 2 = 2**
Did you say 'four minus two equals two?' Good. Did you mean 'If you have four and take away two, you're left with two'? Good.

Negative signs always mean that something is taken away. The result is less than it was before. Negative attitudes also mean that something is taken away. It usually takes away your happiness and your hope. Negative attitudes leave you with less than you had when you started - less happiness, less fun, less good feelings.

Being Positive

"A positive attitude adds happiness, fun and good feelings!"

Positive signs do the opposite. They always add something. For example, read this: **4 + 2 = 6**. Four plus two equals six. You always end up with more than what you started with. Positive attitudes do the same. You always end up feeling better than when you started. **Positive attitudes add happiness, add fun and add good feelings.**

MIND GAMES

The GMH mind works in pictures. If you hear the words 'pink elephant' your mind does not see this in words. It sees a picture of a pink elephant. So you must be careful of the words you hear and say because every word produces a picture.

Try This!

Try this

What does your GMH mind see when you read the word '**Happy!**'

The word Happy

Did you see yourself or another person being happy?

no

Who was it?

—

What was that person doing?

—

Do you now see how your mind works in pictures? no

BOOSTER FUEL

FILL-UP TIME!

Here is another challenge.
How can you learn to think about good things and not bad things? This is what you do!

1. **Choose to feed your eyes with positive pictures.**
2. **Choose to fill your ears with positive words.**
3. **Practice thinking about the 'BOOSTERS!' you see and hear.**

What are 'BOOSTERS!'?
'BOOSTERS!' are pictures or words that help you to become a better person. 'BOOSTERS!' make you (and other people) feel inspired. 'BOOSTERS!' encourage you to be the best you possible. 'BOOSTERS!' are the best things you can feed your mind, your eyes and your ears.
Some examples of 'BOOSTERS!' are:

Words that are true like 'God loves you' and 'you're special'.
Things that are lovely like beautiful flowers and sunsets.
Things that are excellent like top-class athletes.
Things that are admirable like people who help others.
Things that deserve praise like good behaviour and hard work.
Actions that are noble like helping someone in trouble.
Things that are perfect like God's love.

GIVE YOURSELF

When some people feel down and bad about themselves, they treat themselves poorly. They eat junk food, they drink sugary drinks, they stay up late and they end up sick. They tell themselves that they can't do anything right, and they make sure that they don't. If you are like this, stay tuned for some help.
If you meet kids who don't like themselves much, you might see some of these tell-tale signs:

- Jealous of others.
- Can't say anything nice.
- Can't receive a compliment.
- Can't give or receive hugs.
- Often criticise others and compare themselves with others.

Don't be unkind to them. Kids like this already have some challenges to overcome. Try to say something good about them whenever you can.

However, there is one person who could always be a challenge in your life. This person may put you down at least once a day! Who is it? You!

Never put yourself down. Never speak badly about yourself. Instead, treat yourself to a few 'BOOSTERS!'

Think about the good things in your life and talk to yourself with encouraging words. Try saying the things that God says about you on the opposite page. Be a good friend to yourself. Be kind!

FIGHT THE MISERIES

If your thoughts start to wander into the miseries, resist! Fight bad thoughts with all your might. Refuse to be dragged dowr Pour in some BOOSTERS quickly. Take action and take control!

A BOOST!

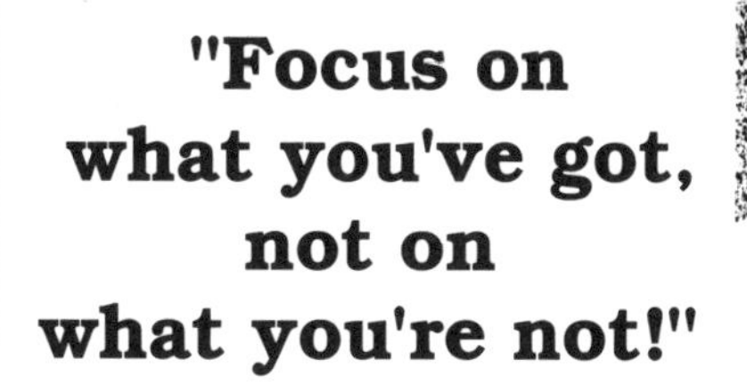

Try This!

Challenge

See how long it takes for you to memorize what God thinks of you and say it without looking.
Start timing now!

I am special.

I am loved.

I am forgiven.

I am cared for.

I am valuable.

I am one-of-a-kind.

I am a winner.

Time taken: 30 sec.

MUD BUSTING!

How to avoid bad fuel

Would you let a mechanic put mud into the fuel tank of your family's car? No way! If he did that, the motor would get clogged up and could not run. Did you know that if someone calls you an unkind name, or talks to you about awful things, they are pouring bad fuel into you. It has the same effect as mud in a motor. You end up with a muddy mind.

You don't want a head full of mud, do you!?

When unkind things are said it is very easy to feel down or mad. But GMHs can do something to put a stop to those feelings.

Here's a little secret for GMH s - whenever you hear an unkind word, hold your nose for a moment. It will remind you not to 'breathe' the mud into your mind. It also helps to remind others not to speak negative things around you.

"When people say negative things about you, they are usually wrong."

Here are three ways you can resist getting a muddy mind from others. **It's called MUD-BUSTING! Mud-busting means staying positive!**

1. **Work hard to ignore the bad things people say. Don't take offense.**
2. **Choose not to hang around with people who gossip, lie and pour mud.**
3. **Pour some 'BOOSTERS!' into your mind. If someone calls you an unkind name, think of four good things about yourself.**

If they say this: **"Hey beanpole! You're skinny!"** you could think of four 'BOOSTERS!' about yourself, like these:

1. I can run fast!
2. I am not overweight!
3. I look good in my jeans!
4. I am going to be the school's best high-jumper!

Have fun MUD-BUSTING!

TAKE TIME TO

Flat Battery?

When a car is running poorly, it may chug, splutter or simply stop. When a GMH is 'out of tune' or feeling low, there are special signs. Sometimes the first sign you see is tears; sometimes a few tears and other times lots of tears. Crying is an important part of being a God-Made-Human. It is not just okay to cry, it is good to cry. Both boys and girls (men and women) need to be able to show their feelings. Tears have a big job to do! Without tears, sad feelings will get dammed up inside you. That's not healthy for your mind or your body. So let the tears fall. A good cry is a healthy thing! It can be the first step to recharging your battery.

"Never go to bed angry."

Hint: But also avoid having to go without sleep for weeks.

Feeling Low

What are some other signs of feeling low?

discouragement?
anger?
crankiness?
sulking?
self-pity?
no energy?
irritable?
no control of your emotions?
temper?

RECHARGE

Try This!

Describe how you behave when you feel low.

Tired angery sad I cry alot

What behaviour would help you to get revved-up again?

Some camephlimps to be and play with friends

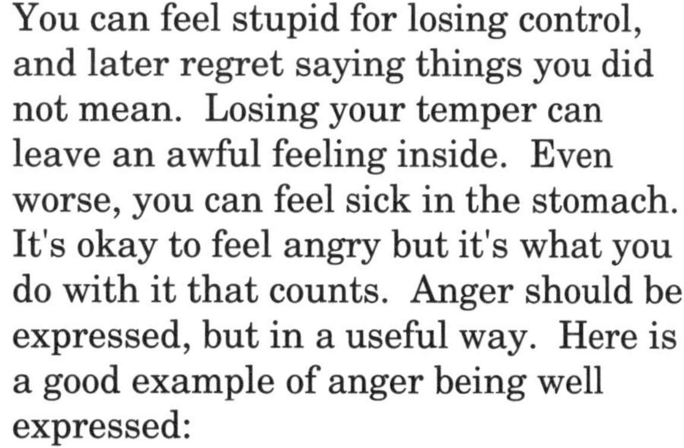

You can feel stupid for losing control, and later regret saying things you did not mean. Losing your temper can leave an awful feeling inside. Even worse, you can feel sick in the stomach. It's okay to feel angry but it's what you do with it that counts. Anger should be expressed, but in a useful way. Here is a good example of anger being well expressed:

"Mum, I feel really angry when you ignore the good things I do and just pick on the bad. Could you please try to praise me too."

Recharge Rules

1. **Take some time on your own.**
2. **Have a good cry if you need to.**
3. **Admit how you feel. Talk to God and write it down.**
4. **Choose to take control (to be back feeling good quickly).**

BEING THE

How to Fix it!

When something goes wrong and you feel low, it's important to fix the problem and not just your feelings.Let's learn how to be mighty problem solvers, especially where other people are involved.
Take time to think about what happened. Ask yourself **"what went wrong"**? and think about what is causing the problem. Try to put yourself in the other person's shoes and think about how they might be feeling. Start looking for an answer.

Admit it when you have made a mistake. Don't be afraid of the little repair job ahead of you. Ask yourself these tough questions and admit to whatever you have done. Remember, you can't fix something until you spot the trouble.

Have I been selfish?
Did I lose my temper?
Have I been dishonest?
Did I take something that wasn't mine?
Did I say something that wasn't fair?
Did I create an argument?
Have I been rude to my parents?
Am I feeling angry with a friend?
Did I tell a lie?

MECHANIC!

FIX-IT TOOLS are for repairing GMH relationships and feelings.
Two of the most powerful words that you can say are "I'm sorry". This can be the start of healing a hurting relationship. Learn all the FIX-IT TOOLS and use them as often as you need to. Add any others you know to this tool kit.

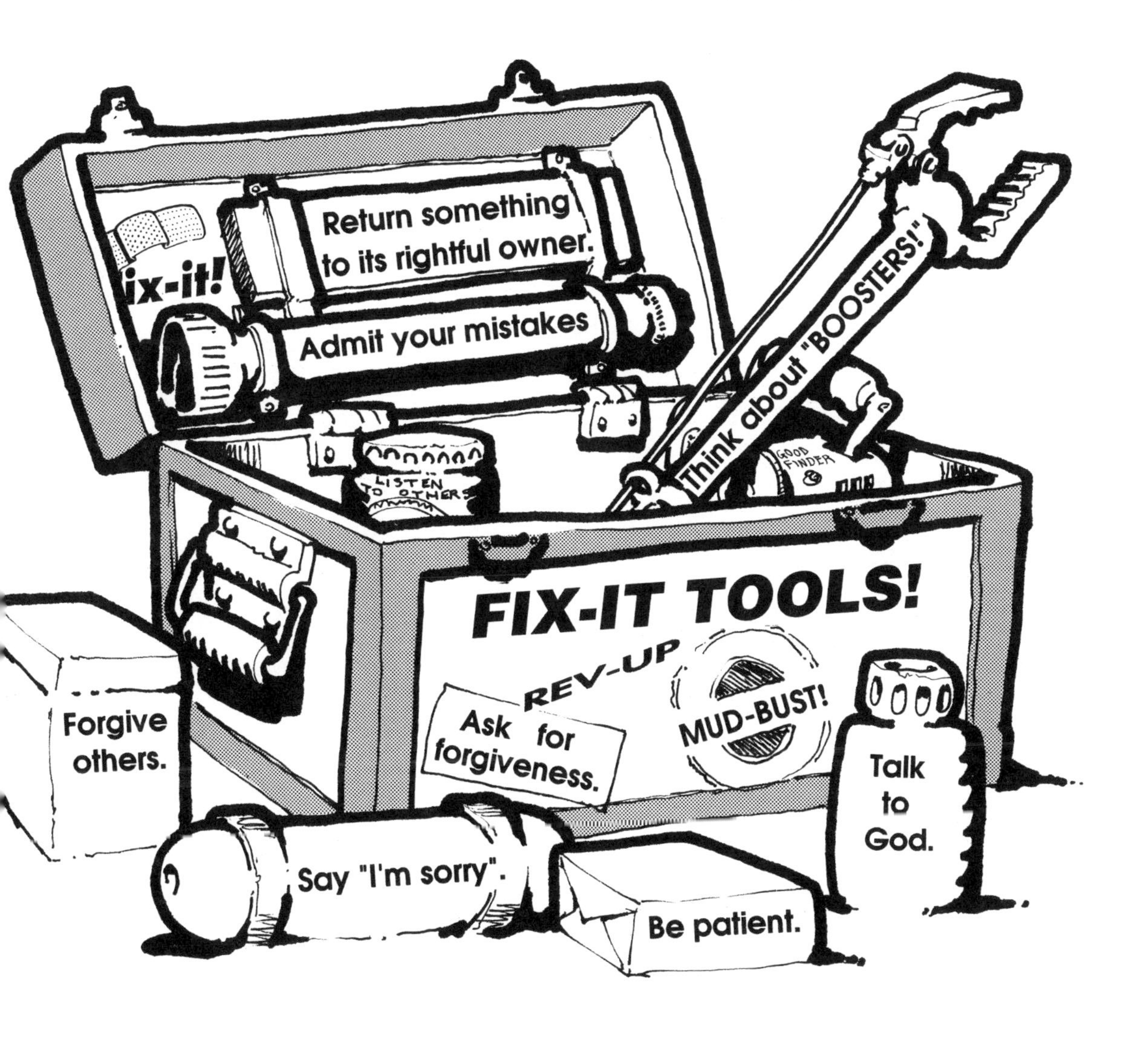

REPAIRS plus HEALING TIME = HAPPY AGAIN!

TAKE CHARGE!

Meet the kids below. Read the things they say about themselves. Circle any statements that you think are true about you.
Highlight any statements that will describe you in the future.

"If it is to be it is up to me!"

I don't like my looks.

My life is boring.

I wish I was like ....

I accept my looks.

My life is interesting.

I am happy to be me.

I gossip about others.

I make fun of others.

I show off to look confident.

I don't want advice.

I boost up others.

I try to like all people.

I am quiet but confident.

I welcome advice.

Ask your parents and friends which person in each pair best describes you. Be sure to write down your answer before they give you theirs.

"I can't".
"I don't know how".
"It'll never work"

I don't like my body.

I'm not good at anything.

I hold grudges.

Other people have all the luck.

"I can".
"I want to".
" I will".
"Let's try"

I'm improving myself.

I'm practising hard.

I forgive myself and others.

Good things often happen for me.

Life owes me a lot.

I've got a bad temper.

Everybody else has fun but me.

Life is what I make it.

I control my temper.

I am a fun person.

I can't because I'm scared.

I can't say what I think.

I'm afraid to ask questions.

I'm too scared to speak in class.

I am bigger than my fears.

I say what is important.

I ask questions no matter what others think.

I make myself try even when I'm scared.

KEEP RIGHT...

DO THE RIGHT THING

On the previous page, did you circle more statements in the left or right column? Be encouraged to learn how to be more like people on the right-hand side! The RADICAL REV-UP Journal has already shown you a lot of tools which can help you to 'KEEP RIGHT!' in your thoughts and behaviour. Let's look at these tools now to help you REV-UP your life.

'KEEP RIGHT!' Tools

KEEP RIGHT

Fuel up with healthy food.
REV-UP with exercise and activities.
Know you are special.
Be a GOOD-FINDER!
Choose to be happy.
Pour in positives.
Feed yourself (and others) BOOSTERS!
Avoid bad fuels and MUD-BUST!
Take time to recharge.
Use your FIX-IT Tools.

Now you have your 'KEEP RIGHT' tools, but there is still something missing. There is something that hasn't been talked about yet. It is another key to making life fun, successful and revved-up!
It is called responsibility!

.Be Responsible

Being responsible means being able to be relied upon to do the right thing."

If nobody was responsible, nothing would get done in this world. Every GMH must accept responsibility for the things around them. To get the best out of life, start on these areas right now, if you haven't already.

Your body

Keep your body-work sparkling clean.
Never put in too much or too little fuel.
Eat healthy food.
Exercise to be in top running order.

Your clothes

Keep your clothes clean and fresh. (you'll look great)
Always neatly fold your clothes.
Store clothes in the right place. (so you can find them)

Your room

Keep your room clean and tidy. (like your mind)
Make your bed.
Fill your room with inspiring things. (so it's a great place to be)

Your relationships

Make room for some special time with your family and friends.
Plan some fun activities together.
Be patient and loving.
Use your FIX-IT Tools.

Your behaviour

KEEP RIGHT!
Feed your mind BOOSTERS!
Be a MUD-BUSTER!

Your abilities

Regularly practice the things you love.
Ask for help when you need it.
Never, ever stop trying!

notes

Chapter THREE

FAMILY & FRIENDS FOREVER!

FABULOUS

GMH families are fabulous! They are not perfect, but neither are you! They are our window to the world. Every GMH, right from the first one, was designed by God to share life's happenings with others. You find that out when you are alone for too long! The GMH family is God's idea of a team. Every GMH is valuable to their team, no matter what they are like. When you were born, your family was put to the test. You needed them for everything, and you got everything you needed. As you grew up, the love of your family helped you to become who you are today. Family life is not easy, but families are a place to grow and learn.

Your family is the place to learn about the world and how to live in it. It is also the place you can learn about love, which is one of the main reasons God invented families. You can still learn a lot about love, even if there isn't always enough of it in your family. Families can be sad and lonely places when there is no love. However, families can be the best thing in the world when you are loved (even if you don't always deserve it). Make your choice to love your family today.

In your family you always have a choice. You can choose to help others not hurt others. You can choose to solve problems, not create them. You can choose to get along with everyone. Your family is your choice!

FAMILIES!

Find a space on this drawing to write 3 good points about each person in your family. Be creative!

FRIENDS

The value of friends

Every GMH wants and needs friends. A good friend is one of the best things you can have in life. As you grow older, your friends might change. A few special people, however, will become close friends, maybe even lifelong friends. Your close friends will be with you to enjoy all the good times and share your tough times. Make sure you look after them. Good friends will REV-UP each other. (Some GMHs get a bonus when their best friends are in their family!)

Watch the people you spend time with throughout your day. Be careful to avoid people who pull you down (the quicksand crowd!). Find friends who try to be the best GMH they possibly can. Their attitude will be contagious, and it is worth catching! They may be even smart enough to say something nice about you.

"If you are happy you will attract happy friends."

When choosing friends, here are a few important things to remember:

1. **Avoid the quicksand crowd.**
2. **Look for those who try to achieve.**
3. **Hang around the 'GOOD-FINDERS!'.**
4. **Look for people who will work through problems.**
5. **Look for happy people.**

"God-Made-Humans go better with friends!"

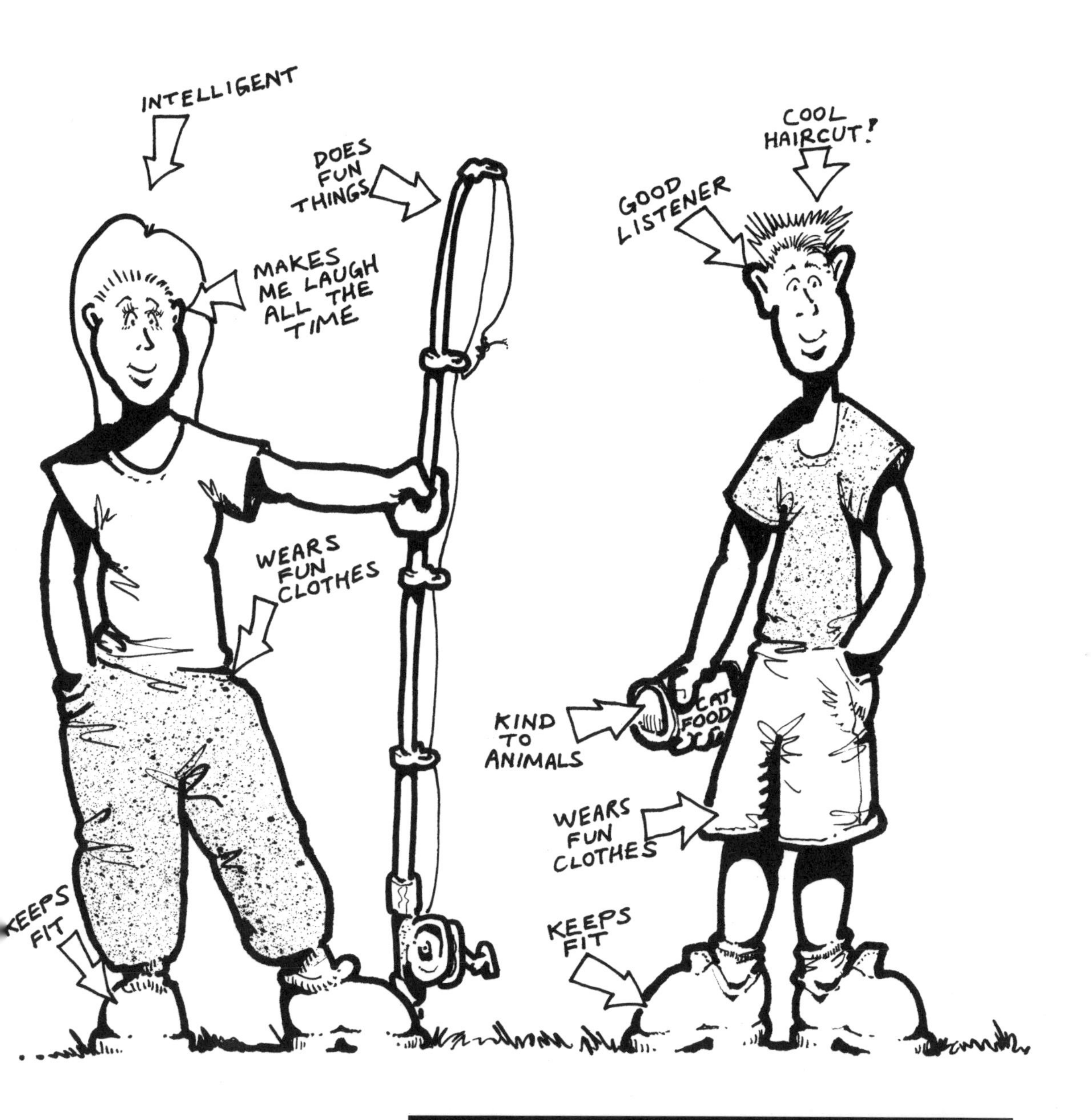

SMILING!

Smiling lets your face know that you are happy. It also helps you to make friends easier. Every smile is like a beautiful gift, yet it costs you nothing to give. You get to feel good. Give them away often!

Challenge

Try This!

What makes a good friend?

List some of the things you like about your friends.

funny
shares things

Challenge

Are you good to your friends? List some of the things that make you a valuable friend to others.

I help when they have troubles.
I don't say mean things.

FRIENDLY TIPS

If you like a friend, let them know it. You can say it, write it or tell them over the phone. But do it often. Imagine how you would feel if every week someone said to you "I'm glad you're my friend". Birthdays and Christmas are a good chance to write and tell your friends what you like about them.

P.S. Parents, brothers and sisters like to hear these things too!

"To have a good friend, you need to be a good friend."

Friendly Tips!

1. Learn to recognise and appreciate what makes your best friends so great.
2. Realise what makes you a good friend to others.
3. Practise ways of being a better friend. You might even ask your friends what they like about you.

WRITE ON!

Time

Out!

Do you know how valuable a letter is? A letter gives you the chance to say something you might not say otherwise. Writing a letter improves your writing and communication skills. Plus - it's great fun sending radical mail to your friends!

5 MAY 1993

Dear Jayne,
Hi!

We went camping last weekend.
Dad took us hiking.

I took my camera and used an entire film.

THIS...

Everyone likes to get a letter. But there can be just as much fun in writing one. Try cutting and pasting, drawing and colouring to add interesting features for a personalised message. You'll soon be creating paperwork that's almost too good to mail!

If you send and receive a lot of letters, why not create a 'LETTERS REGISTER'? You can make a note of anything that arrives in the mail, and also record the letters you send out. Add stamps or fun parts from the mail that arrives!

Here's a tip for finding a pen-friend. Think of your biggest interest (football, fishing, fashion, etc), then go to the newsagent and find a magazine on that topic. Now, simply write a letter to the editor seeking a pen-friend. We are sure they will publish it for you. Good luck!

"Catch yourself saying something good!"

WHAT ARE

What are friends for? Friends are for sharing a part of your life with. Sometimes friends need to help each other to stay revved-up! There will always be people who need help. They could be friends, family or other relatives. We all need to give love and assistance to one another. Sometimes we need it too!

Try This!

Try This!

How do you feel when you help somebody?
I feel useful.
I forget about my own problems.

Try This!

How do you feel when someone has helped you?
I feel liked.
I feel grateful.

FRIENDS FOR?

"The more you give, the more you receive!"

Challenge

Think about your family and friends. Do you know some people who need extra help or care? Plan ahead! Write the names of those you would like to help in the future.

Try This!

Write down your ideas about what our world would be like if nobody helped anyone else.

There would be lots of anger. People would feel lonely and unloved.

CAN PARENTS

Are you friendly with your parents? Sometimes parents forget what it was like being a young GMH. They can get so busy doing other things that they don't spend as much time with you as they would like. Another challenge for parents is having to make the rules at home. Their rules might not be exactly as you would like them, but it is important to respect your parents and obey them.

Parents grow up and have to act like adults (and they don't always want to do that!). They have to work to earn the money to feed and clothe themselves (and you!) and they also have to provide a place to call home. The fact is **... parents don't find this easy.**

Look for ways to help your parents. When you do something with your parents it gives you a chance to talk and build a friendship. Think of some new ways that you can begin to REV-UP your friendship with them today!

BE FRIENDS?

Parents at Play

Parents are big, but there is still a little person inside them. In many cases, they did not want to grow up. It just happened. All of a sudden **- zip! -** and they're adults and all those 'serious' things are zooming through their lives at 1000 kilometres per hour!

So, they forget. Some adults forget how to laugh and play, and where to find snails. (As all kids know, it is very important to watch snails and the way their eyes roll up and down on those wavy poles.) And parents don't have the benefit of a REV-UP KIT like this to help them.

Because many parents worry about their work and their children, they stop playing, laughing and snail-hunting. Instead, many of them sometimes over-eat, smoke, drink alcohol and get tired, grumpy, overweight and then feel even older!

Bring your father a snail today. Kick a football to your Mum. These games are good for parents, and help remind them that they are still kids at heart. Show them that they are your friends.

You can be a better friend to your parents by being thoughtful, polite and by doing the jobs that are asked of you. It takes team-work to make a happy home. Every GMH must do their bit and that includes parents as well.

GRANDPARENTS

Introducing the oldest friends you have ... grandmothers and grandfathers!
They may be older model GMHs that move slowly, but they are fun to be with, have a lot of love to share and can even be revved-up! Most kids will outlive their grandparents by a lot of years. Be thankful for every living grandparent you have!

Grandparents are like a big library for your own family. They are a fantastic source of information, wisdom and handy hints. They are wonderful story-tellers and are living links between you and your family's history.

Go and see them often. Spend time together and listen carefully to what they say. Ask questions. Tell them about the good things you've done. They love to hear it. In most cases, grandparents are very pleased to spend a lot of time laughing and talking with you.

If you have a grandparent living far away, write to them and become pen-friends. If you don't have any grandparents left, adopt one! Think of an older person who interests you, and ask them if you may visit from time to time.

Old people know the value of good friendship and have the time to share it with you. So park yourself next to an older model GMH. You'll be surprised what you will learn!

ARE GREAT!

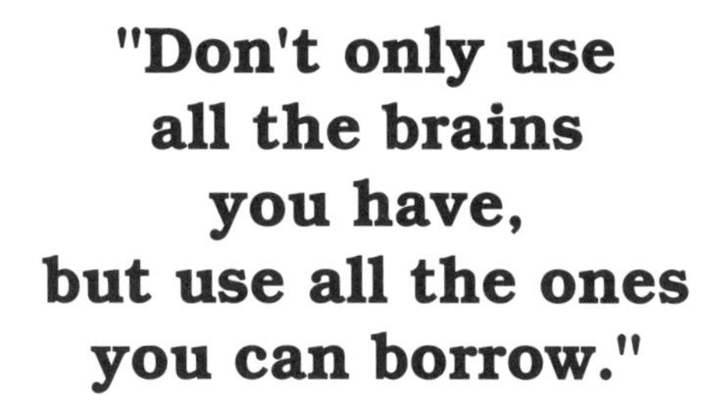

"Don't only use all the brains you have, but use all the ones you can borrow."

Bright Idea!

Get a small hardbound notebook and start recording things after visiting a grandparent. They have plenty of stories, recipes, jokes and witty sayings to tell you. Your notebook will grow into an interesting piece of history that your parents will also enjoy looking at.

WE ALL NEED

It doesn't take much thinking to realise that we all need other GMHs. The 'thing' we need most from people is love. We all need to be loved and we also need to be able to give love.
Love is caring for someone even when you don't feel like it and they don't deserve it. Think of some of the times when your parents have loved you.
Love is caring for someone as much as you care for yourself (or even more!).
Love is a decision.
Love is something you choose to do.
Love is not just saying "I love you" even though that is very important.
Love is showing that you care through your actions.
Take time to think about the people you love. It makes you feel good inside.
It's your choice to love someone. They don't have to love you back.

PEOPLE

Try This!

Encourage others to hug you by hugging them first.

The people I want my hugs from include:

Every body needs praise. Praise encourages us to be better at everything we do.

The people I like to receive praise from are:

Hugs

We all need hugs but not every GMH is comfortable receiving them. Hugs are a great way of showing people you care for them. They are also one of the best things you can receive from people who love you. If you want to get better at receiving hugs you have to practise. As you hug someone, think about all their good points. This makes hugging easier.

Time Out!

NO PLACE

"A home is as happy as the people in it."

It is a big wide world we live in. Full of adventure, challenge and exciting new things to learn. But at the end of the day, we all like a place to come home to. Home is somewhere to feel **safe** and **loved**; somewhere to feel **comfortable** and **relaxed** in familiar surroundings.

SPOT-O

Look closely at this family and spot the answers.

1. **Whose shed is it?**
2. **Where is the arrow?**
3. **What happens if you keep kicking a door open?**
4. **How many bare feet can you actually see?**
5. **Save what?**
6. **Who owns the van?**
7. **How many items are on the clothes line?**
8. **How can you do better homework?**

You'll find the answers on page 154. (but only as a last resort!)

LIKE HOME

HOMEWORK STUDY PLAN
BOOKS ARE MEN'S HEARTS IN OTHER MEN'S HANDS
FAMILY TREE
HOME SWEET HOME
SURFERS
BALI
KIDS ON BOARD

PLAYING THE

Every family needs to work together, like a sports team. Your home needs a set of rules so that everyone can live and play together safely and happily.

If a player breaks the rules in sport, the umpire penalises them. At home, your parents are **the umpires!**
Not all families have the same rules. When you visit a friend's house, you must play by their rules. If you don't, you may get sent home.

Family Rules

Here are some of the rules that Lisa and Roger grew up with.

LISA'S FAMILY RULES
(As made by umpires Pat and John)

Say "Please" and "Thankyou".
No swearing.
Use your manners.
Do not talk over other people.
Apologise before you go to bed.
Never hit or hurt another person.

ROGER'S FAMILY RULES
(As made by umpires Marj and Alex)

Don't slam the doors.
Wash Tiger's dinner dish.
Never ever steal.
Discuss how you feel.
No fighting allowed in the house.

GAME!

Your Turn!

What are some of the rules in your home? Your Mum or Dad may enjoy helping you make this list!

..............................'s Family Rules

Watch Your Manners!

Manners don't come naturally. You have to learn them and practise them. When you use good manners, people tend to like you, listen to you and help you. So REV-UP and put your best manners into action!

HELPING OUT

What about your home? It doesn't matter whether it is brand new or a little tired, your home is the centre of family life. Every GMH is responsible to help make ordinary houses into very special homes. Everyone has a part to play in taking care of the home.
(Except the pets. "Tiger never lifted a paw around our place," says Roger.)

When Lisa and Roger were growing up, these are some of the jobs they did each week.

Try this!

Some homes are very unhappy because all the jobs are left for one or two people. Do you want to be radical? Do you want to shock your parents, while increasing the happiness in your family's home? Think of some new jobs you could do. Write them down here and then ask your parents if you can add them to your existing jobs list. They should be pleased!

Bright Idea!

New Jobs List

Here are some reminders , just in case you are having trouble coming up with good job ideas!

Personal

Make my bed.
Hang up my clothes.
Put away my belongings.
Keep my room tidy.
Put dirty clothes in the laundry.

Family

Set and clear the table.
Wash and dry the dishes.
Pick up things around the home.

TV - THE TIME

Television can sometimes provide wonderful entertainment, but often it provides 'mud'. Remember your MUD-BUSTING skills from chapter two? You'll need them if you choose to watch TV.

There are so many programs on TV that steal your time and steal your family. They promise a lot but teach you nothing. Some kids can spend 3 to 6 hours in front of a TV each day and wonder why they can't get along with their family. They wonder why they're not doing better at school and why they're not very good at anything. TV is not only stealing their time, it's stealing their brain. They could be spending one hour each day on their favourite sport or hobby. They could be spending one hour each day with their friends or family. They could be doing something great! Instead they are watching TV.

Not only that, they are watching heaps of things that don't help them. They watch people being put down and marriages breaking up. They see kids fighting and friends arguing.

They watch losers! None of these things help build a happy home.

So choose carefully what you watch. Only pour in good fuel.

"Whatever you watch, you think about...

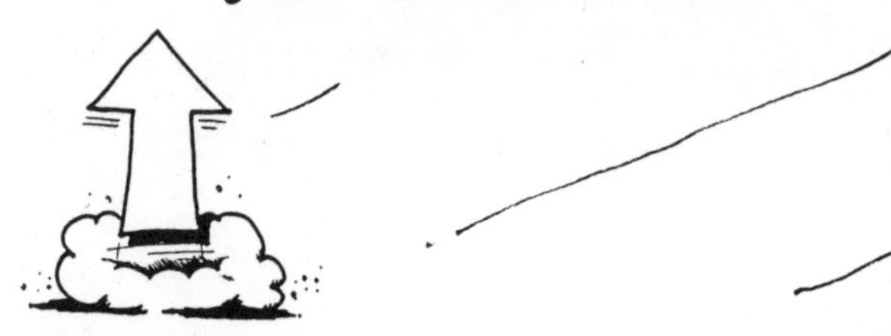

STEALER

...Whatever you think about, comes about!"

TV HEAD

Once upon a time, in a lounge room not very far away... there sat a boy, staring at a box. It stared back, sending noise and light and radiation into his head.

Hours stretched into whole afternoons and late nights plus hours snatched in the mornings before school. All this time they both squatted and stared at each other. At school the boy talked to other GMHs, usually to describe things he'd seen on the box.

That was all he wanted to talk about. He avoided the games and adventures the others played after school. Instead he would race home to sit in front of the box. He didn't particularly care what was on its screen, as long as it was plugged in, switched on and transmitting and that he was sitting before it.

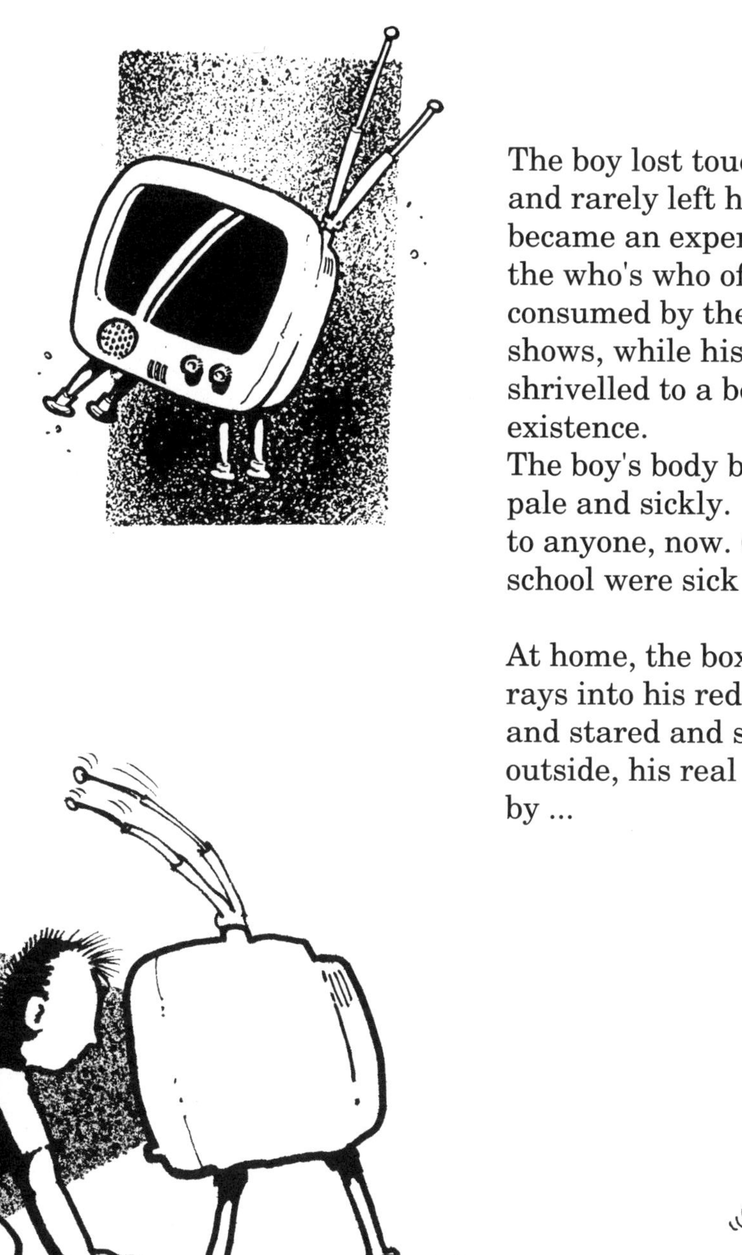

The boy lost touch with several friends, and rarely left home on weekends. He became an expert on game shows and the who's who of 'soaps'. He was consumed by the goings-on in these shows, while his own life gradually shrivelled to a boring little shell of an existence.

The boy's body became flabby, his skin pale and sickly. He didn't speak much to anyone, now. (The children at school were sick of his "TV-speak".)

At home, the box continued to pour its rays into his reddish eyes. He stared and stared and stared, while quietly outside, his real life passed distantly by ...

A POSITIVE

Create your own "positive environment"

Most of us do not choose our environment, which includes our home, our school, our playing spaces and our suburb. We merely go along with the surroundings we find ourselves in. This can be dangerous, because our reaction to our environment is to think, act, and talk like those around us. We copy those around us even when we don't mean to. This means we can easily pick up bad habits!

Your bedroom (or part of it) may be the only space in the house that you can control and decorate. Make sure it is inspiring!! In fact, make it so good that every time you look at it, it makes you feel great! Be very choosy! Don't copy negative friends.

You might like to choose some of the following to put around the room:

Your goals (in pictures or words).
Your dreamboard.
Pictures that encourage you.
Pictures of people you admire or would like to meet.
The good results you expect at school.
Positive words from great books.
A list of your strengths and talents.

ENVIRONMENT

When you control your environment it helps you to control your moods. For you to bring change in your family, you need to be in charge of yourself. The harder you work at this, the better you'll become. Soon you'll be making a big difference in your family.
So REV-UP!

Smile

Smiles are contagious. The person who is happy can always share a smile. If someone doesn't have a smile, give them one of yours. Smiles are like boomerangs. They come back to those who give them out.

BUILD A

Is there more than one young GMH in your family? Having brothers and sisters is great. Not everybody has them, so make the most of yours if you do. Choose to love them and treat them like a best friend. You'll be amazed how well they'll treat you in return.

Keys To Life

Choose to be a friend.
Choose to KEEP RIGHT!
Choose to forgive.
Choose not to fight.
Use your Fix-it Tools.
Solve problems together.
Be a GOOD-FINDER!

Try This!

What are the things you like best about your family?

What things do you find most challenging about living in your family?

Ask your parents and brothers and sisters how they would answer these questions.

BETTER FAMILY

There is no family without problems and challenges. Because every GMH is different, there will always be challenges. But these can bring a family close together. Solving problems is everybody's responsibility. Each person can decide to do everything in their power to build a better family. When you start, others will follow. When times get tough don't give up. Each day do the things that count. Take up the challenge to build a better family!

"You're either part of the problem or part of the solution."

Keys To Success

Listen to others.
Share your feelings calmly.
Help others.
Talk during meals (don't watch TV).
Never go to bed angry (Fix-It first).
Be a problem solver.
Be responsible.
Speak out lots of BOOSTERS!

notes

Chapter FOUR

DESIGN YOUR OWN LIFE!

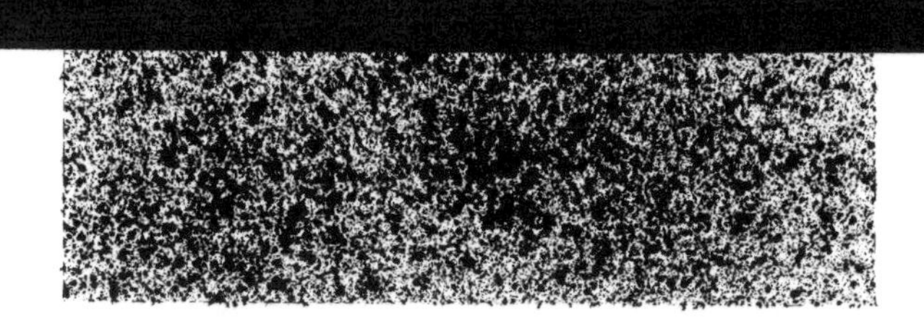

YOUR LIFE IS

Choose what you want!

Deciding what you want in life can be very exciting. There are thousands of things to do and have. There are hundreds of different ways to live. You get to design your own life by choosing the things you like to do, like to be and like to have. In fact, life is very much like a smorgasbord.

A smorgasbord is a feast where you can choose from many different foods and eat as much as you like. First you take a walk around the tables and look at all the different foods. Looking for your favourites, you also keep an eye open for new dishes that you would like to try. There is a limit to what you can eat, so you choose carefully.

"How do you eat a smorgasbord? One bite at a time!"

YOUR CHOICE!

If you try to eat some of everything, you will be too full to move. You may even feel sick. You will also miss out on some of your favourites because you have no space left.

Just as you learn to choose wisely at a smorgasbord, you must learn to make good choices for your life too. Everybody has to make choices, every single day. Why? Because there is not enough time to do everything. Learn to choose the things that are most important to you, first!

DO IT TODAY!

Make a Choice

Your Turn!

Try this!

Ask yourself: **"What would I like to do today?"**

Ask yourself: **"What things MUST I do today?"**

Write your answers down in the space provided below so you won't forget anything.

What do I want to do today?

What things must I do today?

Every GMH should have a list like this for each day of the year. **It helps us to do the things that count most and stay revved-up!**

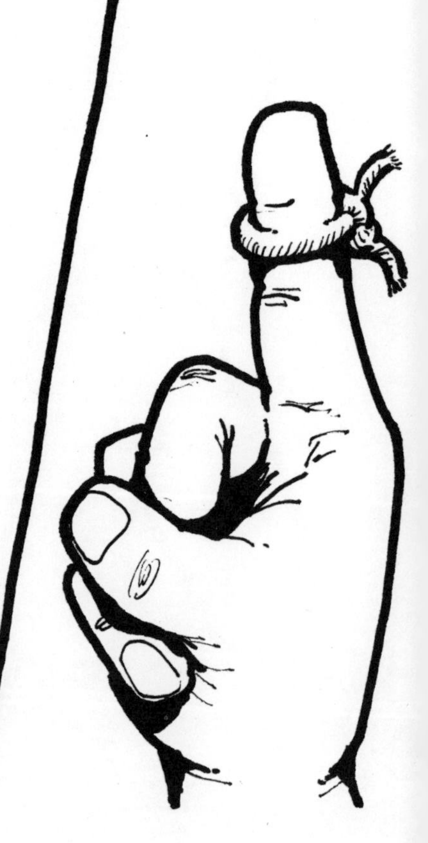

See the 'To Do' list below. This sample page is for you to copy or photocopy and use each day. You'll feel revved-up each time you mark off all the things on your list!

REV-UP

'TO DO TODAY!'

Number each task in the order it needs to be done

Things I'd like to do:

Things I must do:

A little bit done every day makes for a successful life.

WHERE DO YOU

It's time to make your own GMH plan

To drive a car or ride a bike, you first need to know where you are going.
You look at a **map**.
You find your **destination**.
You work out how you are going to **get there**.
You might choose the **fastest way** ...
... or you may choose the **scenic roads**.

Having planned the trip, you take the map with you and head on your way. Brrmmm! No problems.

If you did not look at the map or plan your journey, you might drive or ride around in circles for hours. You might even get lost.

In everyday life, you can also choose where you want to go. You can make plans and map out your future. You can 'see' where you are going if you want to. Most people who don't plan, don't mean to fail, but they usually do. They simply have no known way to get to their destination.

Unless you plan, you may end up somewhere you did not want to go. So REV-UP and plan away!

WANT TO GO?

"Most people don't plan to fail, they simply fail to plan."

TIME TO DREAM

"This GMH is Ready!"

Planning is really a lot of fun and we are going to start right now. Select the first note page and read the title, "Things I would like to own". Quickly write down a few things you would really like, and don't put any limits o your thinking. WRITE THEM DOWN NOW!

In the same way, complete all eight note pages according to each title.

The school results I would like to get

Hobbies I would like to try

Adventures I would like to go on

Lisa: *A trip to the moon!*

Roger: *Camping in Africa!*

Sports I would like to play

SWEET DREAMS!

Do you ever dream?
Do you dream about the future and how you would like your life to be?
Do you dream about being great at something?
Do you dream about being happy?
Deep inside each of us God plants dreams. Good dreams! Awesome dreams! He plants ideas that are exciting and wonderful. God has a marvellous plan for your life. It's better than anything you can think of or imagine. God wants the very best for you. But He does not force it on you.
God has not made you like a robot, who cannot think. You are not like an animal who lives by instinct. You have been given intelligence and the POWER OF CHOICE. You can think and you can decide for yourself.
The POWER OF CHOICE is awesome!
You can choose how you want to live.
You can choose to be happy or sad.
You can choose to love or hate.
You can choose to give or take.
You can choose to help or hurt.
You can choose to succeed or fail.
You can choose to be the best GMH or the worst.
But you get to CHOOSE!

Today is the time to choose to be happy. It's also the time to start dreaming about the future. Dare to dream big dreams! No dream is too big for God and you as a team. Just dare to dream!

"There are three simple words that ensure success. CARE, SHARE and DARE!"

Beware of Dream Stealers

There are dream stealers everywhere. They are people without a dream. They are not happy people and they don't want you to be happy either. Having a special dream for your future makes you feel wonderful. Your dream is a precious possession, so stay revved-up and don't let anybody steal it!

BIG DREAMS!

Dreams are wonderful! They can take over your GMH mind for a while and make you feel great.
Have you ever looked out the window during a class and started daydreaming? Your mind escapes for a while and takes you on a journey somewhere away from school.
Some dreams are more useful than others. Daydreams can be fun but can also be time wasters, like when you dream about things you don't really want to happen. The useful dreams are the ones that show you how your future could be. Your mind spends time thinking about your hopes for the future then starts painting pictures of them in your head. These pictures or dreams are of something you would really like to happen. Maybe you see yourself winning an Olympic medal or being in the top basketball team in the league. It's possible that you see yourself as a singer, a TV personality or a movie star. You could even see yourself as a famous scientist, a writer or a concert pianist.

"If you have a dream, you can make a dream come true!"

Have you ever dreamed of being the Prime Minister or President of your country? All of these dreams are possible. Some people your age are going to fulfil these roles. Why not you?
It might seem so far away right now, but if God has put that dream inside you then it is worth dreaming about. It can make today exciting just thinking about your dreams.

Dream Board

Sometimes when a GMH gets down to some serious dreaming a book is just not big enough. Why not make a felt or cork noticeboard where you can pin up your dreams so you can easily read them and add to them regularly? Have some fun with your Dream Board.

YOUR BIG

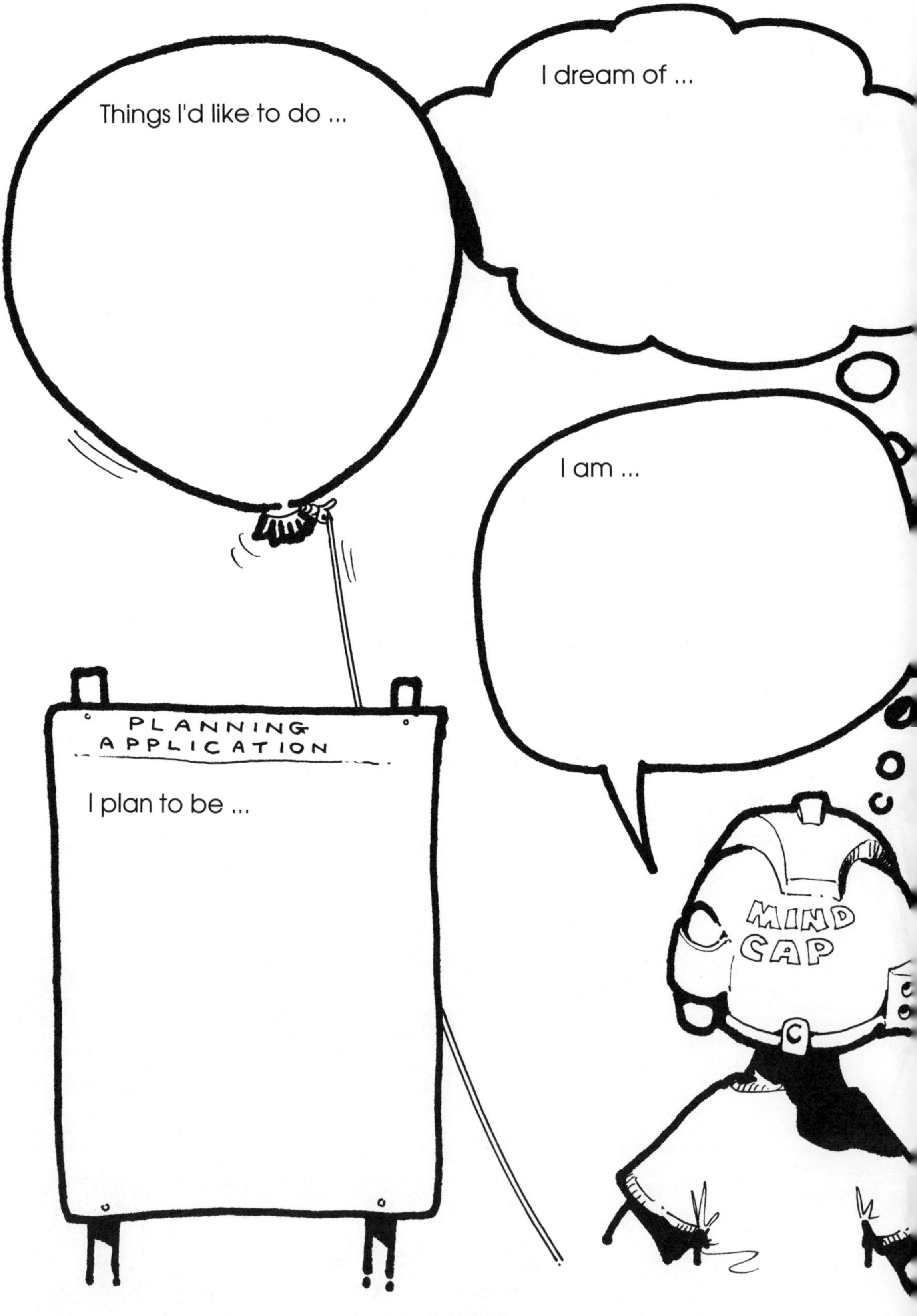

Things I'd like to do ...

I dream of ...

I am ...

PLANNING APPLICATION

I plan to be ...

MIND CAP

DREAMS!

Fill up these spaces with your dreams for the future.

TRAVEL

Now that you are on a road to adventure, why not get excited about future travel. Do you want to go hiking for a day? Would you like to go to the Antarctic for a year?! You can do it! And the first step is to make a plan.

Our world is an exciting adventureland just waiting for your special brand of GMH discovery. Use these unique REV-UP maps to plot your past and present journeys. Don't forget the REV-UP lists to capture all the important details of your plans. Watch out world ... here we come!

On Location

Using different coloured pens:
Mark the spot where you live now.
Mark any places you have been before.
Mark the places you would like to go.
(See the maps on the next two pages as well).

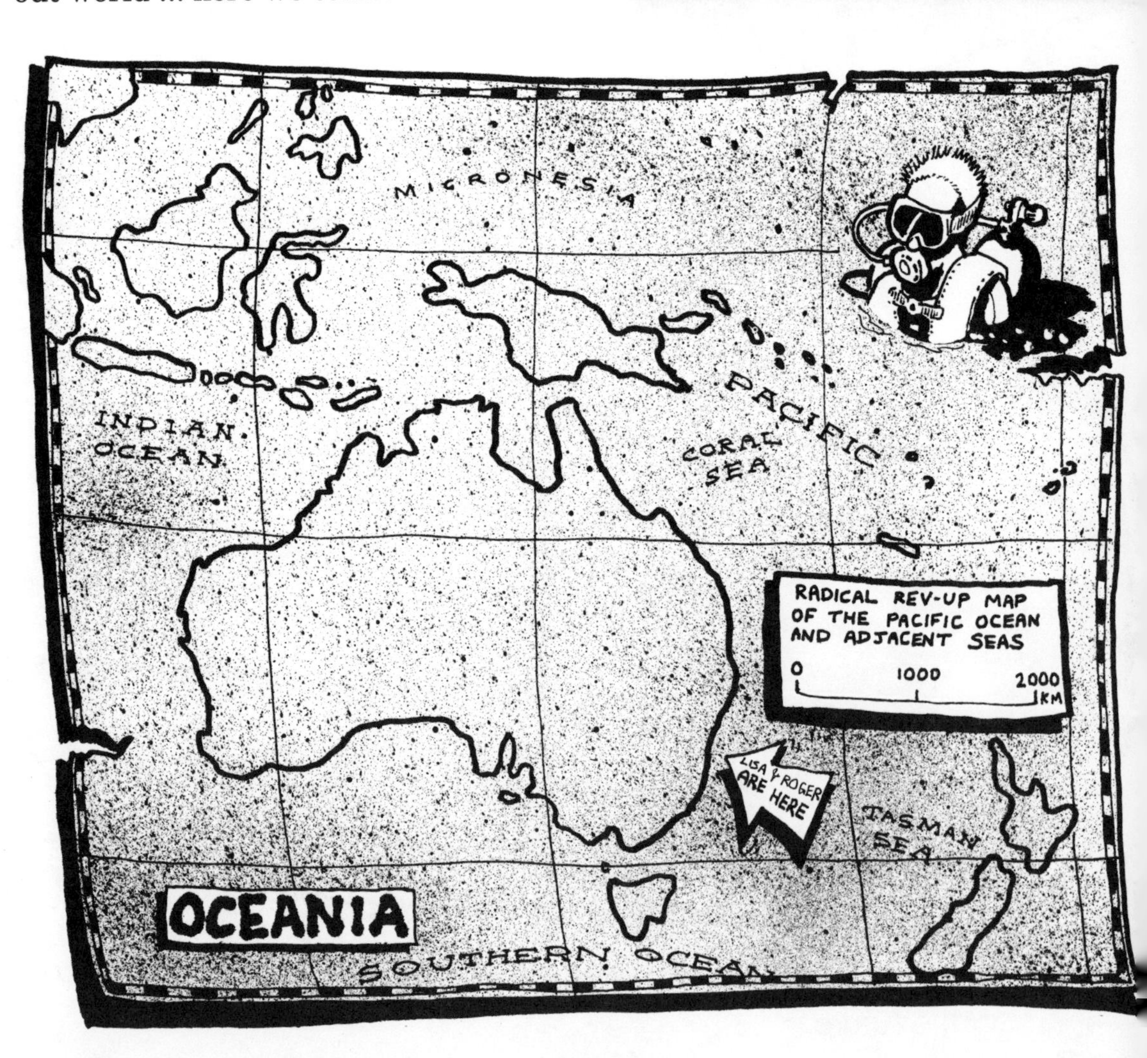

DREAMS

Time
Out!

GET'S COLD UP HERE!
AMERICA
GOOD FINDER
PROMIT
THE SKY'S THE LIMIT!

TRAVEL DREAMS

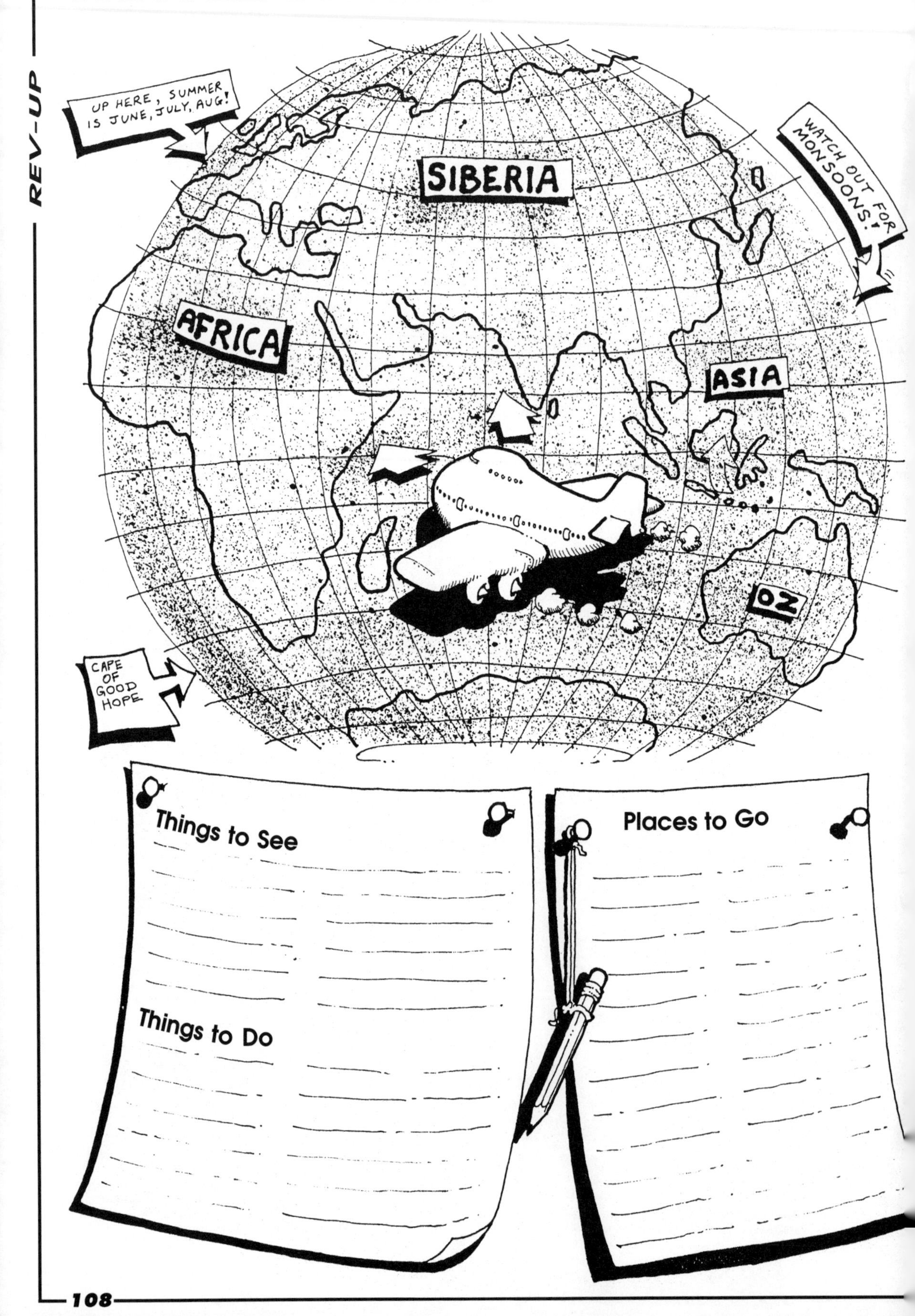

VERY COLD HERE!
NORTH SEA
ATLANTIC
EUROPE
YET ANOTHER ACE AND ACCURATE RADICAL REV-UP MAP.
1 2 3 4 500
KILOMETRES
MEDITERRANEAN SEA
IF YOU ARE HERE, START SWIMMING!
What to Pack
REV-UP
АЭРОФЛОТ
Soviet airlines
ДО TO MOSCOW
MOW
SU 170827

WHAT IS

A Goal Is:

Something you want to do.
Something you want to have.
Something you want to become.

A goal can be anything you want. NOTE! It's good to have lots of goals!

A goal is something you want so much that you are prepared to spend a lot of **time** and do a lot of **work** to reach it. Goals can be very exciting! Goals can also be painful. You may have to **give up** some other activities to achieve your goal. Ouch!

What is success?

Success is the on-going achievement of worthy goals. You are a successful GMH while you are working on your goals. You don't have to wait until it is achieved to feel successful.

A GOAL?

Why have Goals?

Goals give you a target to aim for every day of your life. Goals make sure that you are getting more revved-up every day. Goals help you to measure your progress each week, each month and each year.

"You can't hit a target you don't have."

Remember: Always Write Your Goals Down

1. You will know exactly what your goals are.
2. You will always see them and not forget what they are.
3. It will remind you to do something towards your goals every day.

GOING FOR

GETTING THERE

Earlier, we talked about the smorgasbord of life. You have probably since dreamed up a delicious selection of ideas and choices for things you want to do, have and see. What you have actually done is this: you have taken the first step towards achieving your goals! Congratulations! You are on your way to success.

Choosing the First Step!

Think back for a minute, and picture the tables of food in our smorgasbord story. Using your imagination, what is the first piece of food you would select if you were at a smorgasbord now? Quickly, write it down.

The food I would eat first is:

What can you picture your second choice of food being?
Quick! Write it down.

The second thing I would eat is:

What does it matter which food you choose first? Simply this. You can't start eating until you know what to start with. The same rule applies to any choice you make in life. You can't start walking until you take the first step.

"Whatever you choose to do, do it with everything you've got."

YOUR GOALS

How to Get Started

Now that you are revved-up and have some wonderful goals to achieve, you need to start somewhere. You need to choose a **first step**, then choose a **second step**, and so on. You can achieve your dreams and goals once you make a start. So choose a place to start now!

Can you work on all your goals at once? No! Only one at a time!

Try This!

Select a goal that you would like to start on now. Choose one that is important to you.

1. **The goal I am going to start working on now is**
2. **I want this goal because**
3. **My first step is**
4. **My second step is**

Note: Make sure that you can do each step in half a day or less.

"Ready ...Set ...

Goal-setting is much easier when you divide your life into different areas and choose some goals in each area. Below are fifteen areas in which Lisa sets her goals.

Once you have decided which areas you want to set goals in, you can start writing down as many goals as you can think of. Use the page opposite but also feel free to go back to the pages on 'Dreams' and add more ideas there too.

Try This!

Challenge

Mark the areas in which you would like to set some goals. Add any extra areas that you can think of.

My health and fitness.
My family relationships.
Friendships I'd like to build.
My feelings.
Careers I'd like to try.
New activities I'd like to try.
Things I want to learn about.
People I'd like to meet.
Things I'd like to own.
Places I'd like to go.
Ways I'd like to help in my community.
Books I'd like to read.
Ideas I'd like to work on.
Results I'd like to achieve at school.
Activities I'd like to be great at.

You may like to start your own Success Journal by writing down all your goals in a blank note book. Add to this notebook anything you learn about how to be happy and successful. Whenever you feel miserable this would be a great little book to read!

GOAL!”

You can’t work on all your goals at once, so decide which ones you would like to concentrate on first. Look down your list of goals and number them in order of importance to you. At least decide on your top three priorities.

YOUR SUCCESS PLAN

When you decide on a goal, you need to have a plan to achieve it. The page opposite is a sample of the plan that Lisa uses. You can photocopy this page for each goal you plan to achieve. If you prefer, you can copy this plan into your Success Journal or onto sheets of paper for your Dream Board.

This is easy if you start your goal with "I am ...". Lisa's example: "I am writing a fun book to help kids get revved-up."

WRITE YOUR GOAL DOWN AS IF YOU ARE ALREADY ACHIEVING IT. This is easy if you start your goal with "Iam...". Lisa's example: "I am writing a fun book to help kids get revved-up".

WRITE DOWN WHY YOU WANT TO ACHIEVE YOUR GOAL.
Lisa's example: "I want this goal because kids are really important and I like helping them". (Lisa suggests that you write down ten or twenty reasons if you really want the goal badly.)

"GOAL!"

Photocopy this sheet and use it for each important goal you are working towards.

My goal:

I want this because:

My first step:

My second step:

Possible road blocks:
(problems)

I am prepared to give up:
(For a while at least)

I will need help from:

I will succeed because:

1. I never give up.
2. I can do anything, one day at a time
3.
4.
5.
6.

YOUR SUCCESS

WRITE DOWN AT LEAST TWO SMALL STEPS YOU CAN DO IMMEDIATELY TOWARDS YOUR GOAL. Write these down as if you are already achieving them. If you can think of more steps to do, write them all down. Decide which two steps you will take first. (Make sure that you can do each step in half a day or less.)
Lisa's example: "I am writing five pages each day. I am thinking of three new ideas each day".

DECIDE BY WHEN YOU WILL HAVE YOUR GOAL COMPLETED.
Lisa's example: "My book will be finished by the end of May".

WRITE DOWN ANY POSSIBLE ROAD-BLOCKS OR PROBLEMS YOU COULD COME ACROSS. Be prepared for them so that you will never give up on your goal. (Think about ways you can bust-down these roadblocks.)
Lisa's example: "Some possible road-blocks are:
Not making enough time for writing each day. Letting other work get in the way. People telling me I can't do it. Not concentrating".

PLAN

WRITE DOWN ANYTHING YOU MIGHT NEED TO GIVE UP FOR A SHORT TIME WHILE YOU ACHIEVE YOUR GOAL.

(Remind yourself that you gain more than you miss out on.)
Lisa's example: "I am prepared to give up my free time and my social time for 4 weeks".

7

HELP!

WRITE DOWN THE NAMES OF THE PEOPLE WHOSE HELP YOU'LL NEED.

Nobody succeeds alone. We all need some help. Plan a time to ask these people. (You can't ever have too many people to help you!)
Lisa's example: "I need help from Colin, my Mum and Dad, Colin's Mum and Dad, baby Matthew, Anne, Jan, Sally, Forbes, Melody, Dr. Shayne, Dean and Sandy".

8

WRITE DOWN SIX OR MORE REASONS WHY YOU WILL SUCCEED. Always remind yourself of your strengths and your commitment to your goal.
Lisa's example:
I never give up!
I can do anything, one day at a time.
I have a positive attitude.
I am very happy when I am achieving my goals.
I am a MUD-BUSTER!
I give myself some BOOSTERS every day.

Goals can change ordinary kids into turbo-charged achievers! So REV-UP and GO FOR YOUR GOALS!

notes

Chapter FIVE

BUSTING DOWN ROADBLOCKS

WHAT IS A

Congratulations GMH! You've made it to the last chapter. Now that you have written down your goals and a plan to achieve them, you are on the highway to success.

However, along any road you drive you are sure to come across roadblocks. Roadblocks are obstacles which can slow down your journey. Sometimes they block your road completely like a police barricade or a serious accident. At times like these you have to wait or find another way.

Sometimes roadworks can block part of the road and make you drive slowly or send you on a detour. Roadblocks need not stop you from making your journey, unless you let them.

ROAD BLOCK?

Does a roadblock mean that you have to give up?

Yes  ***No*** 

Don't give up if you run into a roadblock. Let it help you to try harder! Look for a way over it, under it or around it. If you have to, go through it or go another way. But never give up!

A roadblock is a challenge!

It challenges you:

to think
to try new ways
to seek help
to stretch yourself
to learn new things
to succeed!

Every GMH comes across roadblocks. It's what you do about them that counts. Become a great roadblock buster!

WHO CREATES

WHAT'S STOPPING YOU?

Who creates roadblocks in your life? Other people? Yes, sometimes. What about you? Do you create roadblocks for yourself? Yes, of course you do. Most of the roadblocks you have to bust down are created by you. There are two types of roadblocks, self-made and other-made.

Roadblocks

Here is a list of some roadblocks others can create. Can you add to it?

being bullied
having something stolen
being called names

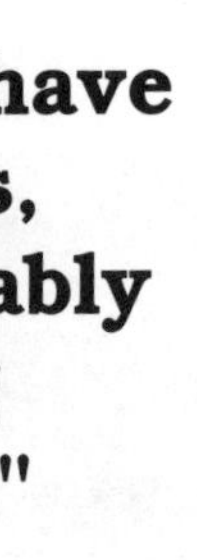

"If you don't have roadblocks, you are probably not going anywhere!"

ROADBLOCKS?

Self-Made Roadblocks

What sort of roadblocks have you created for yourself? Add them to this list.

I make excuses not to try.
I put myself down.
I have a negative attitude.

Let's take a look at how we can bust down the roadblocks in our lives, no matter who has created them.

COPING WITH

Do you know what a put-down is? It is saying mean things about people, or laughing at them in a nasty way. Most of us have been guilty of put-downs. And we have all been put-down by others too!

Put-down targets

Here are some reasons why people may laugh at you, or put you down.

Tick the ones you have been put down for. Cross the ones you have put down others for.

Try This!

- for liking yourself
- for being positive
- for being honest
- for caring for others
- for the way you dress
- for doing poorly at sport
- for not knowing an answer
- for believing in God
- for refusing cigarettes and alcohol
- for crying
- for the way you look
- for speaking in front of the class
- for volunteering
- for defending someone else
- for obeying laws
- for trying to fix a bad situation
- for not giving up

PUT-DOWNS

"Be like cream, always rise to the top."

Are any of these behaviours wrong? No! In fact most of these are good ways of behaving. So why do people pick on them? There are a few reasons. People who don't like themselves find it hard to be nice to others. Instead of trying to improve themselves, they try to destroy other people's confidence and good behaviour. They hope this will make other people do poorly and be like them, so they won't look so bad.
All they really do is get a reputation for being mean. Eventually they lose their friends. We are to feel sorry for people who put down others. They need our love and help.

What Can You Do?

Here are 6 ways to bust down the effects of put-downs.

1. **Don't believe what mean people say about you. Be a MUD-BUSTER!**
2. **Learn how to behave well and always try to get better. KEEP RIGHT!**
3. **Take an 'attitude pitstop'. Tell yourself four BOOSTERS!**
4. **Feel sorry for people who use put-downs. Choose to love them.**
5. **Ask God to help them and you to be kind.**
6. **Always forgive others. Never let their problem become your problem by holding a grudge.**

BORN TO BE

Being different is great! God has made each one of us unique. This means that there are no two people exactly the same. We are meant to be different and our differences make us special. However it can still hurt if you get put down for your differences.
It happens to us all. Here are some of the things that hurt Lisa and Roger when they were kids.
Lisa was born with no muscle in one eyelid. After three operations her eye still looked different. The kids at school called her "ugly" and "bung-eye".
Roger was very fat at school. He was quickly nick-named "heifer-lump" and "hippo". To top it off, he lost two centimetres off his index finger in a motorcycle chain at age 14. Ouch!
Here's what Roger did to bust down his embarrassment about his differences.

Too fat

"I was embarrassed about my weight. My sister told me to stop over-eating and start exercising, so I did. I eventually lost a lot of weight and felt proud of myself! I also tried to join in with the laughter. I would make a joke about my weight to show others I wouldn't be hurt by put-downs, even though I was! It helped anyway."

Missing fingertip

"I lost my fingertip in an accident. I couldn't get that back by exercising! I simply had to learn to live with it. For a year, I kept my hand in my pocket. Then I started making jokes and doing tricks with the finger. Small children were fascinated and laughed a lot. I now think of my stub as a great thing to have, and it's funny too!

"It's better to be looked over than overlooked."

DIFFERENT

What Can You Do?

1. Take an 'attitude pitstop'. See your differences as something that can make you great.
2. Laugh it off! Don't take offence easily.
3. Know your good points and give yourself some 'BOOSTERS!'
4. If you can, do something about it! (Exercise, for example)

If you are embarrassed about a part of your appearance, work out how much you are prepared to let it upset you.
Do you want to WORRY about it?
Yes, a lot Yes, a bit No

Would you prefer to get over your embarrassment?
No thanks. I prefer to keep worrying.

Yes please! I prefer to be confident!

Laugh at Yourself

A good way to bust down these put-downs is to make fun of your own differences. If you do this:

1. People will get sick of teasing you, when they can't upset you.
2. Others will like the way you are able to see yourself in a humorous way. Most people love a good sense of humour.

"Laughter is the best medicine!"

DEAR DIARY ...

Tips for keeping your own personal journal

It has been said that people who write diaries are permanently excited about life. The personal diary is a place for escaping to, and writing about the things that interest you. Your diary is a place to express special feelings and record day-to-day events.

Some good reasons to keep a diary:
Diaries become reliable references.
Diaries help you to learn about yourself.
Diaries are a place of refuge, where you can express yourself.
Diaries are a good place to practise writing.
Diaries are real books made by you!

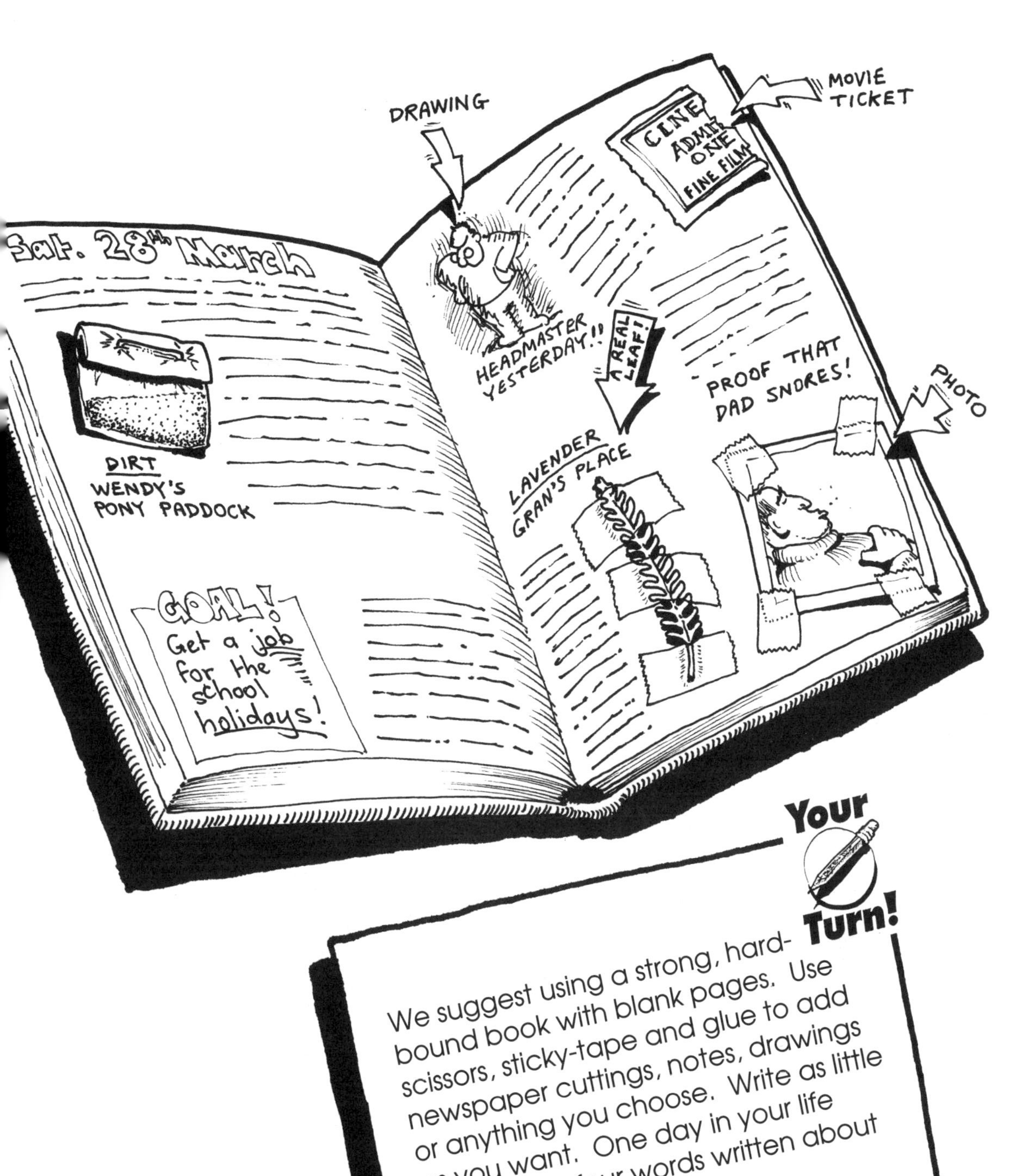

Your Turn!

We suggest using a strong, hard-bound book with blank pages. Use scissors, sticky-tape and glue to add newspaper cuttings, notes, drawings or anything you choose. Write as little as you want. One day in your life might have four words written about it - or four pages!

A word of caution

Be careful. Don't include anything you wouldn't want others to read.

FEAR

What is fear?
Fear is being scared of someone or something that we think is dangerous or evil. It is a roadblock that protects us from a bad situation or a person. It warns us not to be alone with strangers or not to go somewhere alone. Fear can help us to make wise choices.
If you are scared of someone, or a situation, tell someone immediately.

Imaginary Fears

You can also have imaginary fears. Sometimes you can be scared of something that might happen in the future or scared of how others will react. Fear is a roadblock when it stops you from doing something because of what other people might think. Have you felt this type of fear? Do you get scared? Nervous? Do you wonder "How can I get out of this?". Don't worry, you're not alone! We all have fears and we all have to learn to overcome them.
Here is a list of some common fears that kids face:

Fear of criticism.
Fear of having no friends.
Fear of being laughed at.
Fear of failure.
Fear of parents divorcing.
Fear of the opposite sex.
Fear of classroom tasks (reading out loud or being asked a question).
Fear of being hurt.

"Do the thing you fear and fear will disappear!"

List all the things that you fear. Mark the ones you think you can overcome.

To bust through fear:

1. **Ask God for courage.**
2. **Tell an adult you trust what you are scared of.**
3. **Write down a plan to conquer your fear.**
4. **Have an I-can-do-it attitude.**
5. **Think about some "BOOSTERS!"**
6. **Take the first step!**

Note!
Your roadblock of fear might also be a roadblock of worry! (See next page.)

In the Bible God says "Don't be afraid!" three hundred and sixty six times. That is one for every day of the year, even a leap year. He knew we were going to be scared sometimes. God says that we don't need to be afraid when we learn to trust Him.

WORRY

What is worry?
Worry is the imagining of things you don't want to happen. It's like painting a picture inside your head of the opposite to what you really want to happen.
Here are some of the things that worried Lisa and Roger.

Lisa:

1. **My parents might die.**
2. **I will never be good at tennis.**
3. **Going red in front of the class.**

Roger:

1. **Monsters under my bed.**
2. **Not being able to jump the track hurdles.**
3. **That the school milk would be sour.**

The big problem with worrying (thinking up imaginary problems) is that most of the things we worry about don't ever happen! What a waste of time and thought!

"Worry is like a rocking chair. It gives you something to do, but doesn't take you anywhere."

List some of the things that worry you today.

Worry Wash

Perhaps some of your current worries will fade away as you grow older. But let's not just wait around for our worries to go away by themselves. Let's get rid of them quick! Use these rules to regularly wash your mind out, and remove the things you don't need to waste time worrying about!

Worry Wash Rules

1. **Refuse to think about things that 'might' happen.**
2. **Put a picture in your mind of the best that can happen.**
3. **Decide what good things you can do to make the best happen and DO IT!**
4. **Ask God to take control and expect the best to happen.**

Peace

Peace doesn't mean that you're free from trouble or difficulties. Peace means that you're free from worry about these things because God is on your side. He knows what you are going through. Stop! Be still and talk to God. He will give you peace.

Busting Down TV Hours

Many kids spend a large amount of time in front of the TV, watching programs, videos, or playing computer games. Television has become a major roadblock to becoming involved in other activities.

How do you think television, videos and video games are affecting you today?
Watching TV makes my fitness
better ☐ **worse** ☐
Watching TV makes me think
more ☐ **less** ☐
Watching TV makes my talents
better ☐ **worse** ☐
Guess how much TV you watch:

Weekday: .... hours

Sat/Sun: .... hours
Do you think you are watching too much TV?

Yes ☐ **No** ☐

To bust-down TV hours:

1. **Limit your viewing time to 7 hours or less per week.**
2. **Only watch positive shows that build you up.**
3. **Choose to be very good at something you enjoy and practise often.**

"Whatever gets your attention gets you"

A ROADBLOCK

Try This!

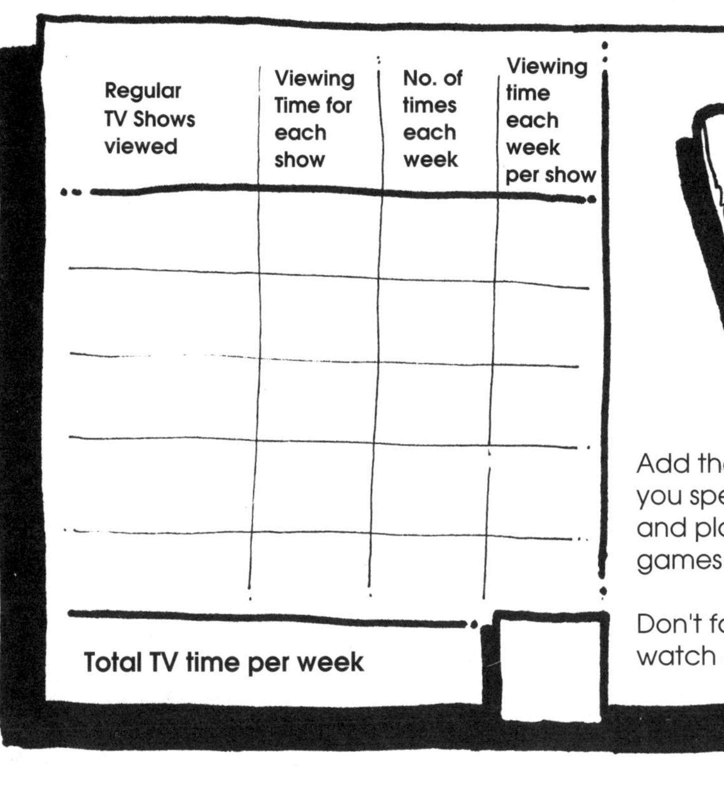

Regular TV Shows viewed	Viewing Time for each show	No. of times each week	Viewing time each week per show
Total TV time per week			

Add the number of hours you spend watching videos and playing computer games

Don't forget the hours you watch on the weekends.

Things I want to be good at	Time spent on each practice	No. of practices per week	Practice time per week
Total practice time per week			

How does being good at something help you?

Choose! What you are going to do with your spare time.

TV or not TV .....

that is the question!

EXCUSES!

Getting Past Your Excuses

Some people create goals for themselves. Others create excuses. We've all made excuses for not achieving at some time. Add some excuses you have used to this list.
I had a cold that day.
She is always brighter than me.
I just can't !

Which sentence would you prefer to be true about you? Circle your choice.

I am filling my life with excuses.

I am filling my life with goals.

If you want your goals badly enough, you'll learn how to get past your excuses and get on with your goals. **Look carefully at your reasons why you want to succeed. Read them aloud seven times.** Watch your excuses fade away as you state your reasons to succeed!

"People who make excuses, make nothing else."

SULKING

Most of us feel like sulking at sometime. Especially if your feelings have been hurt. It's easy to move away from others and have a 'pity party' all on your own. This never makes the problem go away. Often, you just feel worse.

Sulking is like driving up a dead-end street and parking there. There is nowhere to go and the view never changes.

To bust down the sulking roadblock you can do five things:

1. **Write down your complaints and hurts. See them for what they are.**
2. **Ask God to help you deal with them.**
3. **Take an 'attitude pitstop'. Refuel yourself with positive thoughts.**
4. **Decide on a plan to fix your complaints and heal your hurts.**
5. **Take action and refuse to sulk anymore. There'll be no more dead-end streets for you.**

"Be a Grudge Buster! Let go of negative thoughts before they hurt you."

NEGATIVE

Did you know that it is not always what other kids say to you that causes your worst problems, it is often what you say to yourself?
Do you know a person who says "I can't", every time they try to do something? They aren't much fun, are they!

Two truths about 'can't':

1. **No-one knows what they can do until they try.**
2. **No-one knows what they can be good at until they try many times.**

If you want to be able to do something, give yourself between seven and 21 attempts before you decide how well you are doing. (This is how long it takes to develop a habit.)

"TRY plus UMPH! = TRIUMPH!"

Handy Hint!

The next time someone asks you to try something new, say this to yourself ... "I think I can do it!" ... and then have a go!
Note well! If your new activity is more difficult than you thought - DON'T PUT YOURSELF DOWN!
Instead, take an 'Attitude Pitstop' and say: "This is hard but I believe I-can-do-it with practice."

SCREECH!

To become a positive person, you must speak to yourself as you want others to speak to you. If you accidentally say something bad to someone, apologise to them and say to yourself "That's not like me!"

"Be an I-can-do-it person!"

SELF-TALK

Talk yourself into success

Sometimes we are afraid to say we did a good job or that we looked good. But why should we cover up the good things? It is your successes that can encourage others as well as yourself. Don't be afraid to say something is good, when it is. Tell it like it is! And encourage your parents to do the same.

Try these out loud:
I did a good job on my project today.
I behaved very well on camp.
I was proud of how I spoke in class this morning.
I got along well with everyone today.
I felt I improved my reading this semester.
I was the best player in our team on Saturday.

Do you want to be a confident person? Do you know what confidence means? A confident person is someone who is sure of himself or herself. Confident people have a strong belief in themselves. They trust their own ability and believe they can do things well. Is this you? It should be because GMHs are created to be confident. Let's see why you can be confident. Firstly, you can be confident in the one who made you, because He makes no mistakes. Secondly, you can be confident in yourself because you were designed by God. You must be good! Thirdly, GMHs are given dreams and the God-given ability to make them come true. So you can be confident in you!

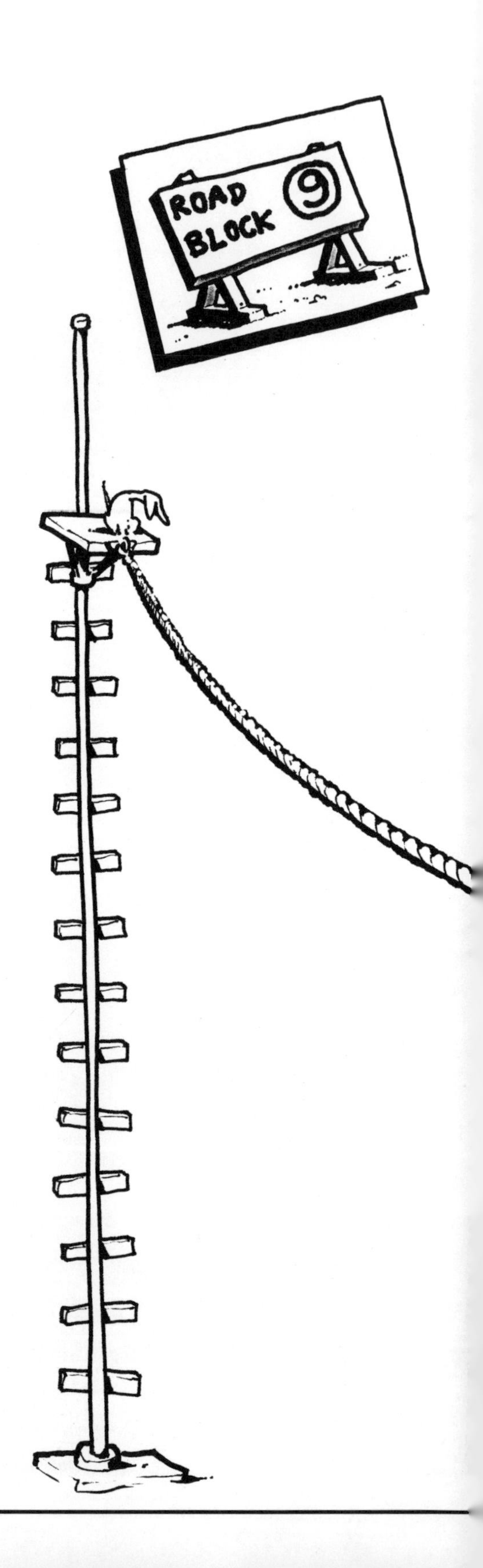

Confidence Wins!

Choose to be confident not because of what you can do but because you will enjoy learning new things more. Here are some more good reasons to choose to be confident:
A confident person can accept criticism.
A confident person can attract friends easily.
A confident person knows he or she may do poorly but is still willing to have a go.
A confident person knows that looks are only skin deep and what counts is inside.
A confident person isn't scared of the opposite sex - they are interested!
A confident person is not afraid to do his or her best in the classroom.
Confident people can handle being laughed at, and know how to laugh at themselves too.

CONFIDENCE

When you're good at something, it can make you feel very confident about yourself. You don't mind if people watch you because you know you can do it well. You trust your own ability. But why wait until you are good before you trust yourself. Be confident first so that you can become good at something faster.

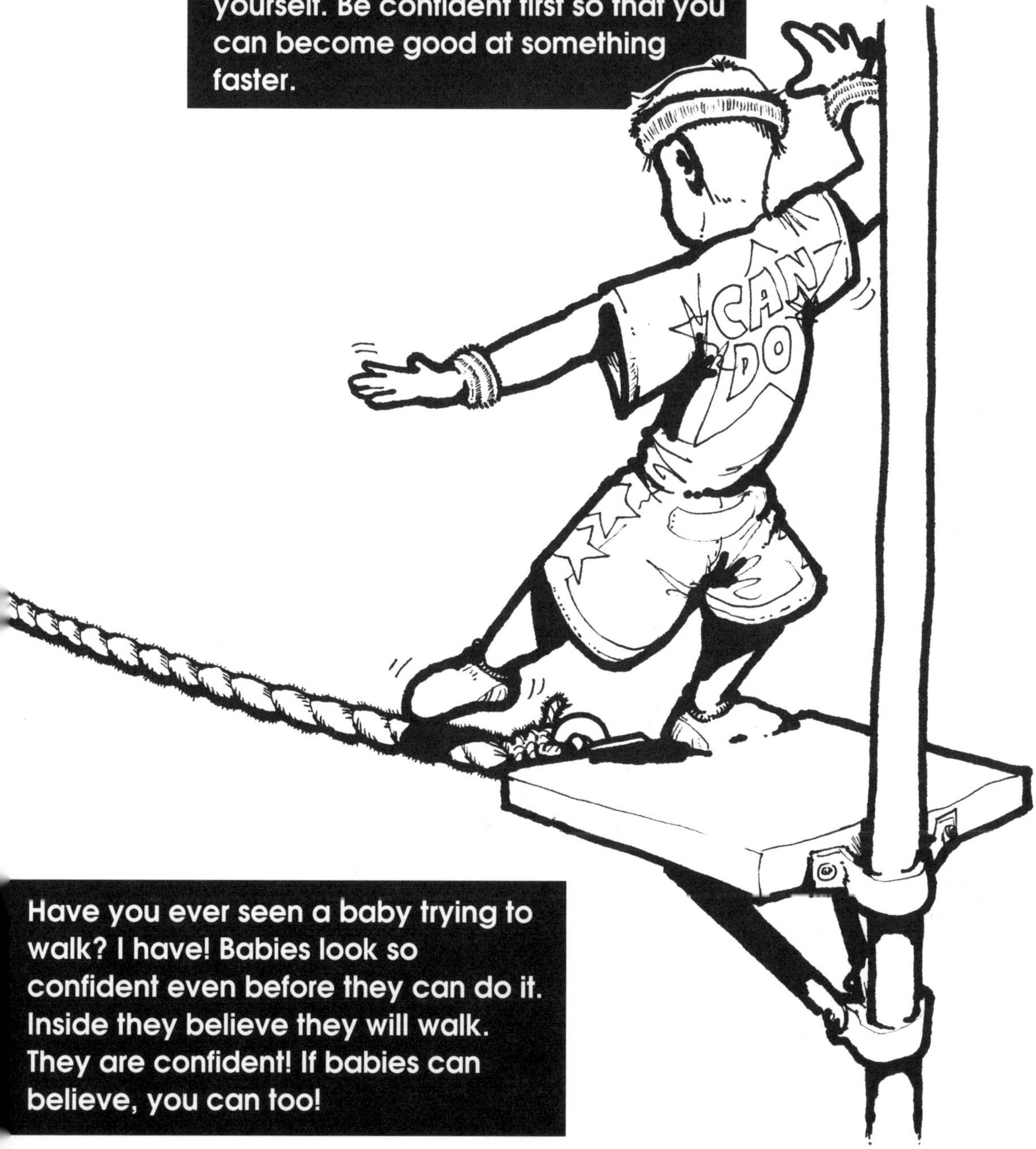

Have you ever seen a baby trying to walk? I have! Babies look so confident even before they can do it. Inside they believe they will walk. They are confident! If babies can believe, you can too!

MISTAKES MAKE

Oops! You made a mistake? Oh dear. What a fool you must be. Aren't you?
NO WAY!
Mistakes are examples of self-made roadblocks. Actually mistakes are a real bonus in your life! They are like little pushes from behind that help you to learn, re-shape your ideas, correct your direction and improve your performance.

"If you're not making any mistakes, you're not doing anything."

If you are making mistakes, that means you are trying new things and going places. When you give your best efforts, you are bound to make a few mistakes along the way.

1. **Mistakes don't have to be roadblocks.**
2. **Mistakes can be 'helpers' to show you where you need to do something differently.**

People who don't make mistakes are often found doing nothing. They may be just sitting around, waiting for the next chance to cast a put-down your way.

Would you like to make no mistakes, if it means not doing much and going nowhere?

Yes  **No** 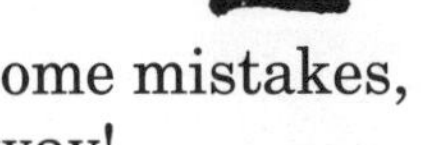

Would you like to make some mistakes, but eventually go a long way!

Yes  **No** 

YOU GREAT!

Think about some of your mistakes in the past. Write them down. Can you think of the ways they may have helped you? Describe how.

Try This!

Mistake

The help it provided.

"Anything worth doing, is worth doing poorly at first!"

Winners versus losers

A winner makes more mistakes than a loser. A loser is someone content to sit back and criticise. Losers let a mistake stop them from chasing their goal. Winners focus on their goal and keep trying no matter how many times they do poorly. Winners know that you have to do poorly before you can do well.

THE PURPOSE

Ouch! You were trying hard, but it began to hurt. Is that a roadblock? Not necessarily. It may just be a detour. Pain has a purpose. It's job is to help you monitor how far you go and how fast. If you're running to get fit, pain will help you to know how much to do. When you feel uncomfortable you know your body is working hard. That's good! When you feel pain, it is probably time to rest and do some more later. Severe pain tells you when your body has done too much, such as a strained muscle. Then you must stop. But wherever there is great effort,there will also be some pain.

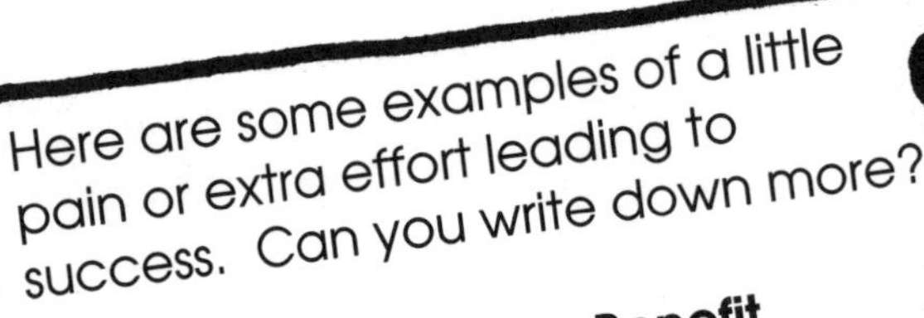

Here are some examples of a little pain or extra effort leading to success. Can you write down more?

Type of Pain	Benefit
jogging each night	win a school race
working part-time	buy a bicycle
doing extra home-work	best in class

OF PAIN!

An Olympic swimmer may swim over 200 laps a day in training. Does it hurt?

Yes  **No** 

A mother can take as long as 24 hours to give birth to a baby. Does it hurt?

Yes  **No** 

A child will fall off a bicycle many times, learning to ride. Does it hurt?

Yes  **No** 

In the examples above, should these people give up when they feel the pain?

Yes  **No** 

Never let pain be a roadblock on your way to success. Use pain to make your GMH better and stronger. What's more, if you pay the price of pain, you will enjoy the benefits of success!

Here are some rules to bust down the roadblock of pain:

1. **Use pain as a monitor of your progress.**
2. **Take an 'Attitude Pitstop' when you are hurting.**
3. **Never give up when it hurts!**

"No Pain, No Gain!"

NEVER A

ACROSS

DOWN

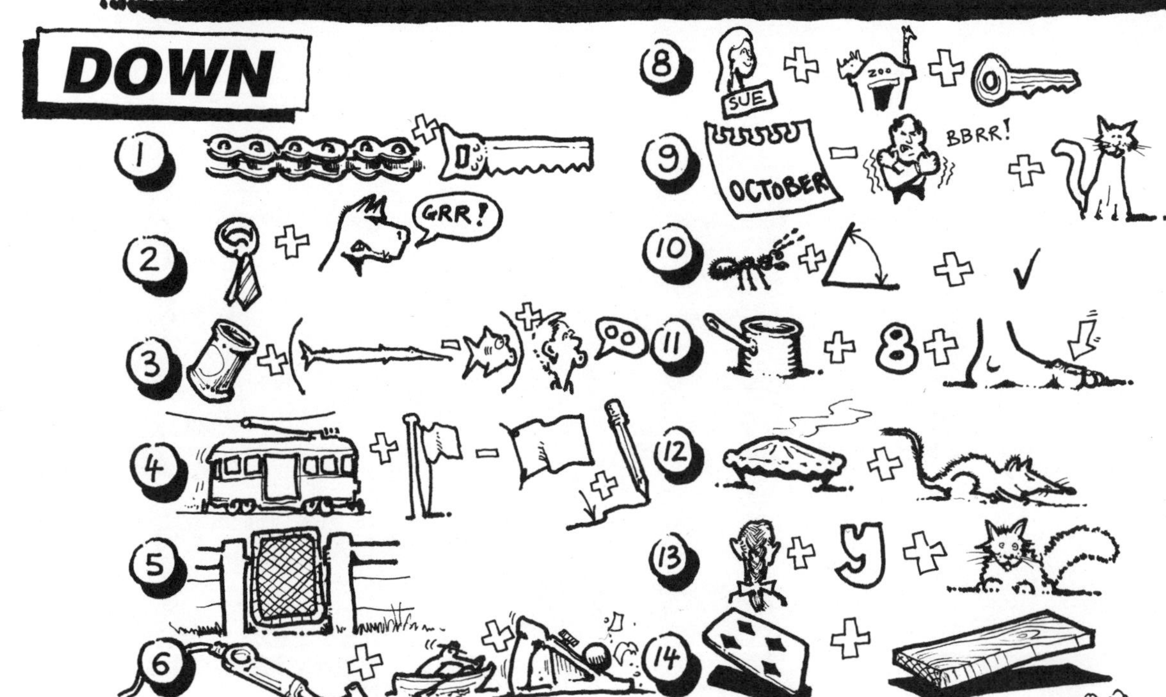

CROSS WORD

Time Out!

A challenging crossword for your revved-up minds!

A FINAL CHECK

Being REVVED-UP doesn't mean you are always moving fast. Being REVVED-UP means that you are inspired to do what counts, when it counts. Often this means taking control of the parts of you that get out of control. There are times when your temper needs to be controlled, as do your moods and your feelings. You must also control what you eat and how you behave.
With the RADICAL REV-UP Tools you can choose to TAKE CONTROL!

How much you control yourself is up to you. It's a choice! But it's not just a matter of telling yourself to do it. You need to build friendships that will support you. You need to develop good habits for when the pressure is on. Lisa has been learning how to do this since she was a kid. On the page opposite are some of the ideas that have made her life happier and more exciting!

"If you do the things you ought to do when you ought to do them, then someday you can do the things you want to do when you want to do them."

Habits

Most of what you do during the day is done by habit. If you repeat a behaviour seven to 21 times, it establishes a pattern - or, a habit - in your brain that you do automatically. Some of the things you do by habit are the way you walk, brush your teeth and speak.
To get rid of a bad habit, replace it with a new behaviour and do it at least seven times and up to 21 times.

UP!

Happy Habits

Write 'I' before the habits that you already do.
Highlight those which you want to improve on.

See inspiring movies.
Read inspiring books.
Learn from educational cassettes.
Sing in the car.
Talk positively to myself.
Take 'Attitude Pitstops'.
Read my goals and dreams daily.
Feed my mind BOOSTERS!
Eat healthy food.
Learn how to live from the Bible.
Listen to inspiring music.

Apologise. (Sooner rather than later!)
Forgive others quickly.
Solve problems as they arise.
Laugh whenever I can.
Write my own Success Journal.
Ask others for help.
Create an inspiring bedroom.
Put my goals on the bathroom wall.
Smile often.
Fight the 'miseries' !
Take time to recharge.
Dance around the house!

Choose friends who encourage me.
Talk to God about everything.
Be a MUD BUSTER!
Play sport.
Do many activities.
Choose to be happy!
Remind myself that God loves me.
Encourage others.
Plan time with my friends.
Be a GOOD-FINDER!
Use FIX-IT Tools.
Love God.
Love others.

IT'S TIME TO

A fun way to remind yourself of the changes you have decided to make is shown below. Draw a picture of yourself (or paste one in) and write down all the things you are going to do with an arrow pointing to the appropriate body part. If you want, you can enlarge it to poster size and paste it on your wall. Then you will be able to read it every morning and night.
The picture opposite is for you to experiment on. You can draw in your own face and hair, and then add your arrows and changes. REV-UP and have a go!

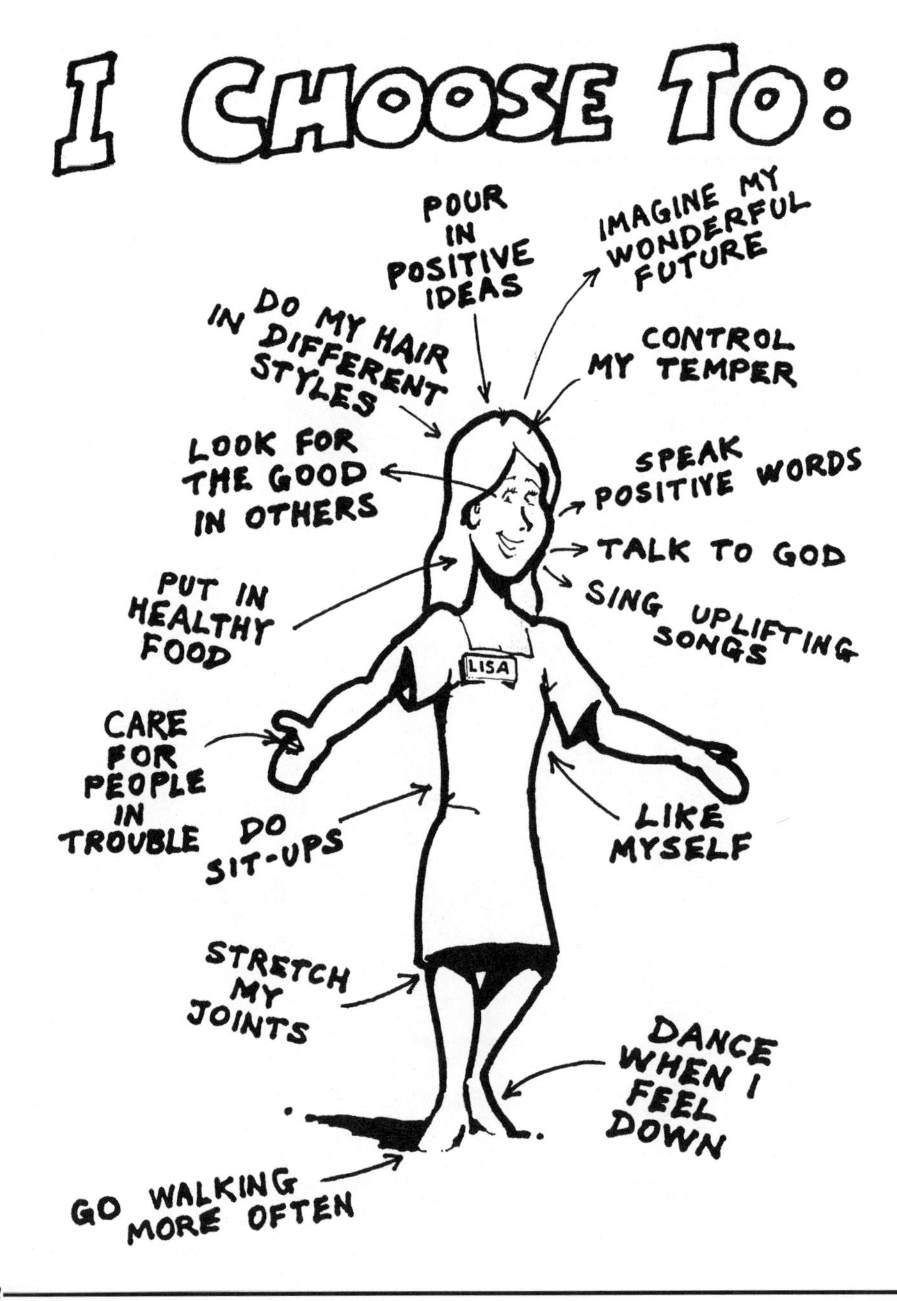

REV-UP!

ANSWERS

How Valuable Are You?

Lisa's answers from pages 16 and 17.

1. YES

You want your GMH body because you can't live without it. And, of course, there are those who want you because they love you! God wants you more than anyone because He's your real owner.

2. NO

You can't ever be replaced because there is only one you in the whole wide world. You are unique and very special.

3. YES

You are worth much more than money. Ask your best friend or a parent how much they think you are worth. They will probably say "Much more than money can buy!". This means all the money in the world could not buy you. Would you sell a leg, an arm or an eye for a million dollars? Of course not! It's easy to see that you are more valuable than a six million dollar man.
God says you are worth more to Him than all the things created on Earth. To prove it, He sent His son Jesus to Earth as a GMH to tell you how much He loves you. Like all GMHs Jesus had to die. But He died for us so that when we die He can take us to Heaven with Him.
Jesus paid the highest price ever for you and me. He says GMHs are worth the most!

4. YES

God loves you!

SPOT-O!

There's No Place Like Home!

1. Dad's shed
2. The arrow is on the roof
3. You will kick a hole in the door
4. Five bare feet
5. Save the whale
6. The van belongs to Dad too!
7. There are three items on the line
8. Use a study plan

Never A Cross Word

Down

1. chainsaw
2. tiger
3. kangaroo
4. trampoline
5. gate
6. aeroplane
7. eagle
8. Suzuki
9. octopus
10. Antarctic
11. potato
12. pirate
13. platypus
14. cardboard
15. farmhouse

Across

1. football
2. dragonfly
3. utility
4. stopped
5. fantastic
6. microscope
7. barbecue
8. spaceship
9. wombat
10. Walkman
11. torch
12. goanna
13. surfboard
14. commodore
15. carpet
16. breakfast

SYMBOLS

This is a quick reference list to understand the meaning of the symbols used in the REV-UP Kit.

Be a '**GOOD-FINDER!**'
(page 20)
Looking for the good in yourself and others.

'**KEEP RIGHT!**'
(page 56)
Always do what you know is right.

Go '**MUD-BUSTING!**'
(page 49)
Stay positive while you bust through mud. (Mud is anything that tries to pull you down.)

Take an '**Attitude Pitstop**'
(page 40)
Stop what you are doing and refuel your mind with positive, encouraging statements.

Use your '**FIX-IT**' **Tools**! These special tools fix hurting friendships and help you become a better friend.

Fill up with '**BOOSTERS!**'
(page 45)
Fill your mind with pictures or words that build you up to be a better person.

'Time Out!'
Take some time out to try a radically different, fun-filled activity!

'Bright Idea!'
An idea worth trying!

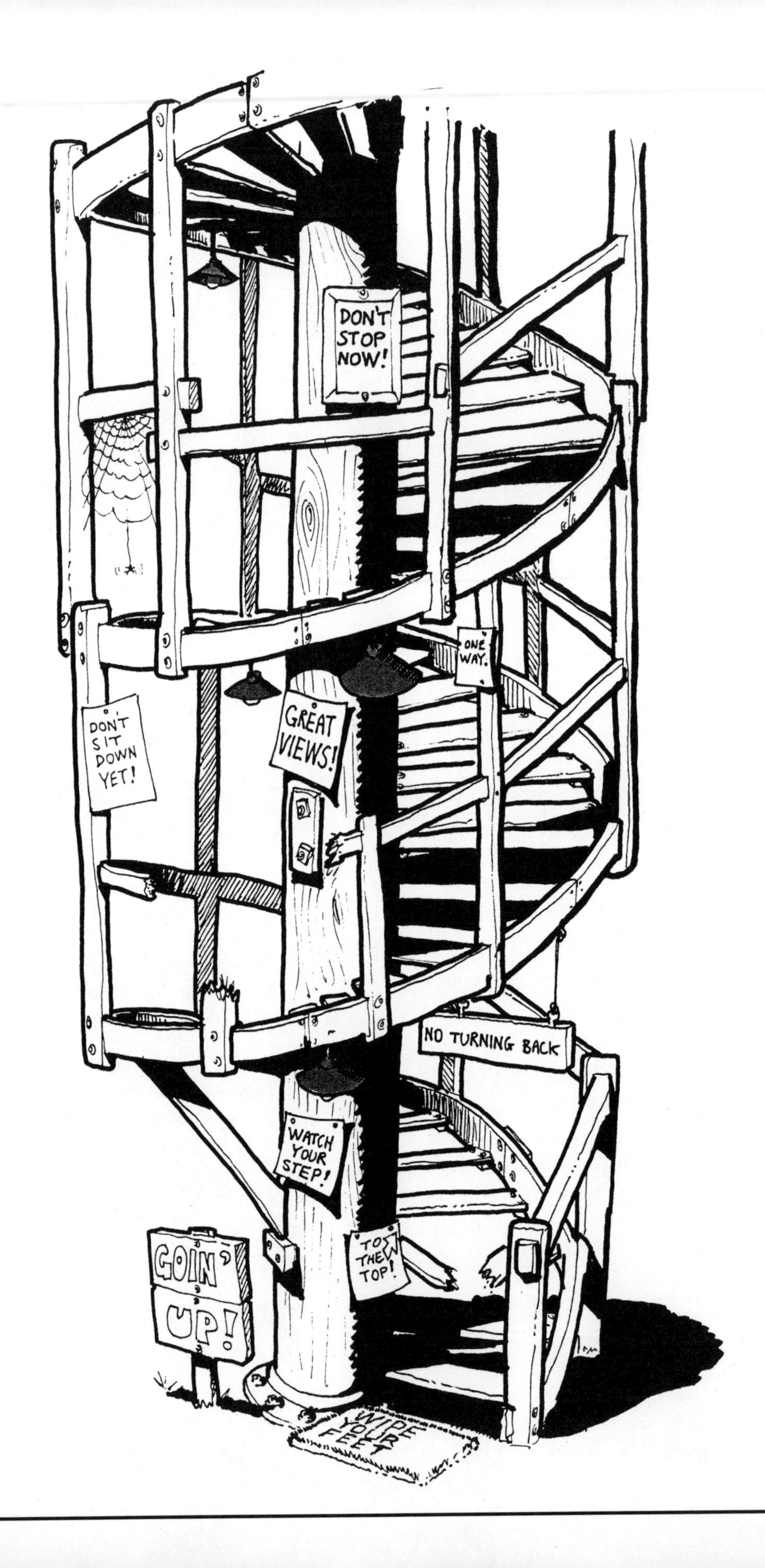
DON'T STOP NOW!
ONE WAY.
DON'T SIT DOWN YET!
GREAT VIEWS!
NO TURNING BACK
WATCH YOUR STEP!
GOIN' UP!
TO THE TOP!
WIPE YOUR FEET

Our Exciting Youth Program!

An Australia-wide network of teenagers going places.
What a great concept! Would you like to be a part of that network?

Motivation

Confidence

Conferences

Fun!

Excitement!

Life-Changing!

Newsletters

Seminars

Outdoor Learning

Self-Esteem

Lisa and her top team of speakers, motivators and trainers have developed a program especially for teenagers. This program is designed to change and grow as you do, as it tackles the important and challenging areas in your life.

Indicate your interest in Lisa's Youth Program by completing the form below and mailing it to:

Cassette Learning Systems
7 Panorama Court
Bulleen, AUSTRALIA 3105

Yes!

I want to go places with the Youth Program!

My Name is: .... **Age:** ......
Address: ....
.... **Code:** ....
Birthday: ....

BE INSPIRED
with Lisa McInnes-Smith

MOTIVATIONAL FLIPCHARTS!

Encourage, uplift and amuse yourself and your friends with these three best-selling desktop flipcharts!

Mood Maker | **Doom Destroyer!** | **Keeping Couples Cooking!**

PERSONAL DEVELOPMENT PROGRAMS!

New! Radical REV-UP Kit for Kids

Inspire confidence, purpose and happiness in your seven to 14-year-olds with this radical new personal development kit!

"Why Wasn't I told?"

Develop confidence, set goals, solve problems and become a motivated achiever through this unique program for teenagers and adults alike!

I'm a Walking Talking Miracle

Help your primary school-aged children to set goals and build self-esteem. This program is life-changing while based on fun-filled activities!

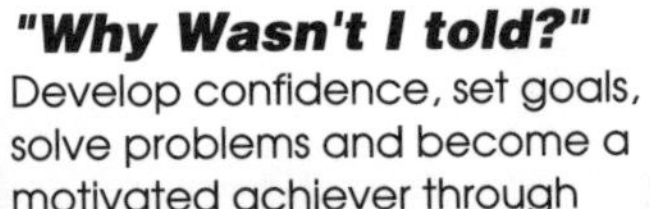

How to Motivate Manage & Market Yourself

Become the winner you were created to be with this all-in-one success book for adults!

Motivating Magnets!

Keep the keys to success always in sight! Two sets of three magnets.

MOTIVATIONAL MESSAGES

Cards for all Reasons!

Keep in touch and inspire those around you with this set of eight cards and envelopes for all occasions!

"Read to Lead" bookmarks!

Set of eight inspiring bookmarks. Let Mr Bookworm encourage your children and friends to read daily!

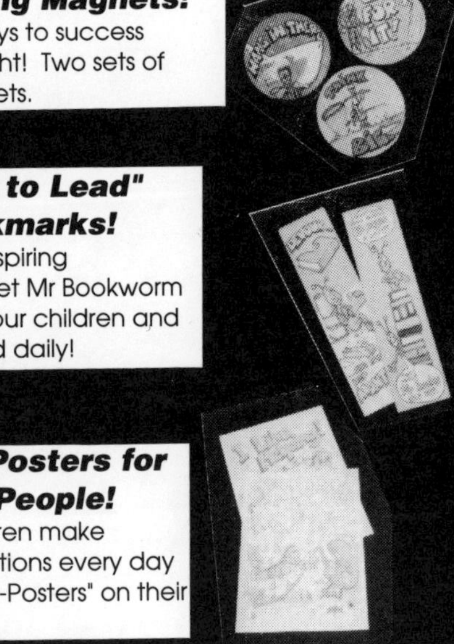

Positive Posters for Little People!

Help your children make positive affirmations every day by putting "Posi-Posters" on their walls!

Positive Postcards!

Encourage and uplift others with a short note to show you care. Pack of 15 postcards with envelopes.

ORDER FORM

LISA McINNES-SMITH has helped to improve the lives of thousands of Australians through her books and cassettes. Children have developed confidence, adults have found purpose and problem-solving skills, while teenagers have found direction and self-esteem.

Lisa began with a dream to help youth. She undertook studies in Education and Sports Psychology and is now recognised as one of Australia's most dynamic motivational Speakers. Lisa is available for conferences. Phone for further information.

To order any of Lisa's Self-Help programs:
Tel: ***(03) 850 1492***
Fax: ***(03) 852 0498***
Or, send this form to:
Cassette Learning Systems Pty Ltd
7 Panorama Court, Bulleen, AUSTRALIA 3105

ITEM	***PRICE***
Mood Maker	*$15.00*
Doom Destroyer!	*$15.00*
Keeping Couples Cooking!	*$15.00*
New! *- RADICAL REV-UP Kit For Kids*	*$40.00*
"Why Wasn't I Told?" - book & 2 cassettes	*$34.00*
"Why Wasn't I Told?" - book only	*$12.00*
I'm a Walking Talking Miracle - book & cass.	*$26.00*
I'm a Walking Talking Miracle - book only	*$15.00*
How to Motivate Manage & Market Yourself	*$20.00*
Cards For All Reasons!	*$15.00*
Motivating Magnets! (per set) *Set A - Do What Counts!* *Set B - Think Big!*	*$13.00*
Positive Postcards!	*$15.00*
Positive Posters!	*$13.00*
"Read to Lead" Bookmarks!	*$10.00*
(postage & handling - normal mail)	*$ 4.50*

I enclose $..........................in payment by Cheque/Bankcard/Mastercard/Visa/Amex
Card No: **Expiry Date:**
FULL NAME: ....
ADDRESS: ....
....**POST CODE** ....
Signature:

I THINK THE WORLD IS MUCH BETTER TODAY THAN 10 YEARS AGO!

HOW CAN YOU SAY THAT? DON'T YOU EVER HEAR THE NEWS? HOW CAN YOU TELL ME THIS IS A BETTER WORLD?